Flash Point of Deceit

Flash Point of Deceit

The U.S.-Dakota War of 1862

By Larry Stillwell

[signature: Larry Stillwell]

Gold Fire Publishing
2719 17th St. S., Moorhead, MN 56560
www.goldfirepublishing.com

Gold Fire Publishing

2719 17th St. S., Moorhead, MN 56560   Phone: (218) 236-1042
publisher@goldfirepublishing.com   Fax: (218) 233-3582
stillwell@goldfirepublishing.com   www.goldfirepublishing.com

Although the author has made every effort to ensure the accuracy of this work, the author acknowledges his literary embellishment of the true story by classifying his writing as a "historical novel."

The watercolors on the back cover were painted by Donna Stillwell.
Front cover design by Knight Printing, Fargo, N.D.
Book design by Julie Sorenson, Creative Copy, Moorhead, Minn.

Publisher's Cataloging-in-Publication
(Provided by Quality Books, Inc.)

Stillwell, Larry E.
    Flash point of deceit : the U.S.-Dakota War of
1862 / by Larry E. Stillwell. -- 1st ed.
    p. cm.
    LCCN: 99-63639
    ISBN: 0-9672709-0-1

    1. Dakota Indians--Wars, 1862-1865--Fiction.
2. Wood Lake, Battle of. 1862--Fiction. I. Title.

PS3569.T478F53 1999   813'.54
                        QBI99-796

*For all her enthusiastic assistance
in editing and helping me
write this book,
I dedicate this novel to
my daughter, Julie.*

*Thanks also to my wife Donna
for her help and encouragement
during the writing of this book.*

John Otherday

The sketch of John Otherday was printed on page 401 in "A History of the Great Massacre by the Sioux Indians in Minnesota," by Charles S. Bryant. Rickey & Carroll, Publishers, Cincinnati. Copyright 1864, expired.

Little Paul

The sketch of Little Paul was printed on page 166 in "History of the Sioux War and Massacres of 1862-1863" by Isaac V.D. Heard. Published by Harper & Brothers, Publishers, New York. Copyright 1863, expired.

Table of Contents

Preface

While serving as an administrator at Dr. Martin Luther College in New Ulm, Minnesota, I became interested in the local history.

Research in the city library turned up a lot of information about the U.S.-Dakota War of 1862. I was incensed at the terrible treatment of the original citizens of the land, the Dakota. As a father, I felt great sadness for parents whose children were crying and dying of starvation. Even as this people group had little choice but to fight back, they knew it was a losing battle. The only thing that could not be taken from them was their proud sense of heritage.

All who were at the flash point of deceit suffered greatly.

Yet, in the midst of the horrors of war, there arose people of courage, character and spirit who saved lives at the risk of their own. I have long been in awe of the stories of John Otherday and Little Paul, Christian Indians whose courage saved hundreds from certain death.

This story has long grown in my spirit, and it is a privilege to share it with you. Decades of research are the basis of this true story. However, because my imagination has filled in the places where facts are not available, it is categorized as a historical novel.

This "Wasicun" has long admired the Native American people, and numbers many friends among them.

I want them to know my heart is good.

Prologue

For two hundred years, the Dakota and the newcomers, mostly fur traders, lived at peace. The trade between the Dakota and the whites made the fur traders rich. In exchange, the Dakota received goods that made hunting and camp life a little easier.

The fact that the fur traders laid no claim to the land probably was the greatest reason why the Dakota tolerated their presence.

The first land grab by the whites came in 1805. The United States government took one hundred thousand acres and paid the Dakota with gifts, liquor and two thousand dollars — two cents an acre.

That "treaty" established a precedent for more unfair treaties in the future.

As more whites pushed into the territory, more treaties were made. Then the government began funneling the treaty payments, called annuities, through the trader stores. It became common practice for traders to present their Dakota customers with inflated bills, or just verbal, fabricated claims against the annuity payment due.

The Dakota had little recourse but to settle for whatever balance the trader allowed them to keep after skimming funds off the top.

In ever-increasing numbers, the whites came; lusting after the rich land, seeking their fortunes. Still more "treaties" were made to rob the Dakota of their heritage.

In 1849 Alexander Ramsey became territorial governor of Minnesota. He and a co-conspirator, trader Henry Hastings Sibley, went to work in earnest. They used everything from flattery to outright threats to get the Dakota to sign over their land. It was "open season" on the Dakota.

More than twenty million acres were taken from the Dakota, who were moved to a reservation -- narrow strips of land on either side of the Minnesota River. Having shared their beautiful, life-giving land and trusted the United States government and its people beyond reason, the noble Dakota were relegated to a fragment of their former glorious domain.

The Washington politicians decided to take care of the "Indian problem" by turning them into farmers. Some Dakota accepted the opportunity as a way to feed their families and cooperated with the staff placed at the Yellow Medicine and Redwood Agencies. They received farm land, homes, outbuildings, tools, supplies and training to establish farms. The Dakota farmers were required to cut their hair and wear white man's clothing.

Other Dakota families firmly held to their traditional ways and could not accept the white man's ways. These traditionalists developed a contempt for the better-fed, well-equipped Dakota, and referred to them derisively as "cuthairs." Occasionally their disdain was demonstrated through attacks on the cuthairs and their property.

Tension among the Dakota, and between the Dakota and the U.S. government grew as annuity payments were repeatedly delayed, food rations were inedible, and hunting lands were quickly depleted of wild game.

Local staff at the two agencies, traders and area settlers were not necessarily the cause of the problems, but by their mere presence they represented the despised U.S. government. Many good friendships developed between cooperating Dakotas and the more respectful whites. Unfortunately, cultural differences and small disputes between the two groups gave everyone a personal laundry list of insults, hurts and grievances against the other. These compounded offenses were the local tinder of anger that would help ignite the conflict which was ready to explode. The situation eventually reached its flash point on August 17, 1862. The embers of the conflagration burn still.

The Warrior

A sudden explosion of birds out of the trees and brush ahead of him dropped Good Sounding Voice to one knee. At the same time he brought his Henry rifle from the crook of his arm to a ready position. Instantly his eyes and ears strained to identify the reason why the birds flushed. It certainly was not a creature of the forest.

To be a Dakota deep into the land hunted by the Chippewa and not be alert was *icikte* — suicide. He had left his pony hidden in some trees in a gully and was scouting ahead, looking for deer sign.

Quietly and carefully, he eased into the brush behind a towering oak tree. He was close enough to the trail to be discovered, and if the intruder happened to be a Chippewa, Good Sounding Voice was in for a fight. Escape was impossible, for the trees were too scattered to cover him in retreat. He eased around the edge of the tree far enough to scan the landscape ahead where the birds had taken flight. A chill went down his spine as he spotted two warriors riding toward him on the very trail that ran right beside him.

They were of the hated Chippewa tribe. Instantly Good Sounding Voice cocked his rifle so they would not hear the necessary click when they drew closer. Moving slowly, he tried to blend himself into the thicket while keeping himself in a position to fire when needed. He wanted them very close when they spotted him so the element of surprise would be in his favor. Good Sounding Voice knew he had to kill them both. There was no other choice. He would kill the lead warrior first and then it would be one-on-one with the second.

Pacing his breathing to match the gently fluttering leaves, he waited as the two drew closer. He dared not move a muscle. He thought that at any moment he would be seen, but his luck held. A gentle waft of air carried the acrid smell of sweat and the raspy breath of the ponies. The warriors were almost upon him. Time seemed to stop as Good Sounding Voice watched the lead warrior turn his head to look right at him. In that same instant, he fired.

The quiet serenity of the forest was shattered as the bullet tore a gaping hole in the Chippewa's chest. The warrior's pony reared in fright at the blast and its already dead rider slid to the ground.

The noise and action startled the remaining warrior's horse and it too reared, pawing at the air over the body at its feet.

Good Sounding Voice sprang forward for a better position to fire again. Before he could raise his rifle, the wild-eyed horse and its rider charged into him, knocking him flat on his back and sending his rifle skidding away from him. Good Sounding Voice looked up in time to see the warrior hurtling down off his horse, his knife drawn and already arcing down in a deadly slash.

By reflex Good Sounding Voice reached with both hands to intercept the attack and caught the knife-wielding wrist. In the same motion Good Sounding Voice brought up his knee into the belly of the surprised warrior and tumbled him over his head, giving Good Sounding Voice time to regain his feet and draw his own knife.

By now the Chippewa was on his feet, slowing circling with his knife thrust out in front of him. Good Sounding Voice went into a crouch and circled to the right with the cutting edge of his knife turned up and his arms half extended in front of him, his powerful legs ready to spring. In a low, guttural hiss, Good Sounding Voice snarled. *Ciktepi.* I kill you.

The Chippewa charged, his knife hand slashing with a stabbing thrust like a striking snake. The point etched a slight cut along the ribs of Good Sounding Voice, who arched back and away from a more lethal contact.

The Chippewa's face registered pleasure, as if he already smelled victory. Then, with a grunt, both leaped forward and collided, each grabbing the knife wrist of the other. They fell to the grass, each trying to break his own knife hand free. They rolled on the ground, neither giving quarter to the other.

Good Sounding Voice, about to have the Chippewa gain the superior position, whipped up his arms, raising the Chippewa high above him. In the same motion he brought his knee hard up into the warrior's groin. The face of fury, which had moments before grinned in anticipation, now fleetingly attested to pain and dumbfounded recognition of defeat. As the Chippewa doubled up and rolled away, Good Sounding Voice broke his knife hand free and drove the blade up under the enemy's rib cage, slicing upward toward the heart. The Chippewa body shuddered and was still.

Good Sounding Voice rose to his feet and stood gasping for air. He watched as his enemy's flayed heart poured out its lifeblood back to Mother Earth. Looking at the massive body, he knew he had been lucky to end it so quickly. The Chippewa was heavier than he. Had the fight gone on longer, it could have ended differently.

Slowly his own heart's rhythm returned to its normal pace as Good Sounding Voice picked up his rifle, cleaned and loaded it, and laid it close by. Triumphantly, he bent down over the cooling corpse of his enemy and grabbed a handful of hair. With a quick circular slash of his knife, he popped the scalp loose and then went over to his first kill to repeat the process. Wasting no time to gloat over his victory, he wiped his knife clean in the grass and returned it to his belt.

Once more astride his pony, hunting forgotten, Good Sounding Voice allowed himself to savor the elation of his victory. The thin scratch on his torso tingled, adding to his electrifying sensation. His medicine was strong, and he had destroyed the enemy. He knew there would be wailing and weeping in the Chippewa village once the bodies were discovered.

Had he not been trapped, he would have let the warriors pass and continued on his way. Good Sounding Voice respected life too much to kill for the sake of killing. He would not hesitate to kill to protect his family and the people of his village, but to seek out someone to destroy was not in his spirit. As a young warrior of twenty summers, he wanted more out of life.

Hunting expeditions rarely are such lively excursions now, he mused, as he finished splitting wood and gave his axe a final thump into the stump. He arched his back and stretched. Recalling that surprise encounter with the two Chippewa always gave him a chill, but the warmth of the morning sun's rays on his back was quickly bringing him back to the present.

John Otherday was now in his forty-third summer, and he no longer rode the warrior trail. The choice game that was so plentiful in his youth seemed to disappear in direct proportion to the growing number of whites invading the valley. Many Dakota, more by necessity than by choice, had become farmers so they could feed their families.

"Cuthairs," they were called by the warriors of the Soldiers' Lodge. It was not by any means a term of endearment. Wearing the clothes of the white man did not of itself make the farmer Indian welcome in white society. On the other hand, wearing their hair cut short to the nape of their necks did much to symbolically cut them off from other Dakotas who resisted any change to their traditional way of life.

John Otherday did his best to live peaceably in both worlds. He was the leader of a small band of Wahpeton farmer Indians, and was himself an excellent farmer. He left the name Good Sounding Voice behind him with his warrior youth, and now Ampatutokacha was his Dakota name. He was disliked by those who had not changed from the old ways, but they respected him enough to not cross him openly.

Whites knew him as John Otherday. His farm was five miles northwest of the Yellow Medicine Agency. As unofficial leader of the farmer Indians in his area, John was a frequent visitor at the agency. He had developed good relationships with the officials there, especially Noah Sinks, warehouse supervisor at both the Yellow Medicine and Redwood agencies. John was married to a white woman named Dawn whom he had met in Washington City when he had gone east with others as a delegate to a treaty meeting.

As part of the federal government's effort to make the region safe for settlement, farmer Dakotas received tracts of land and farming equipment and were taught how to work the land. Good homes were also provided. John's home was built of brick from the kilns of the local agency, and two summers ago the agency added an additional room. Bit by bit, the farmer Indians adopted a lifestyle more closely resembling that of the whites who settled the area.

John stretched once more as he slowly turned, eyeing the horizon where his fields spread across the land in healthy vigor. His crops this year looked better than they had in the last two growing seasons. Satisfied, he turned to the house and crossed the yard which was already beginning to warm under the morning sun. It was the season of the hot moon, August.

Stopping at the wash stand near the door, he dipped some water from the wooden bucket into a basin and washed his hands and face. After returning the towel to its hook on the wash stand, he picked up the comb lying next to the basin and ran it through his hair before stepping into the kitchen.

John was greeted by his son and the smell of freshly baked biscuits which Dawn prepared 'most every Sunday morning.

Little Wind, his son of seven summers, was already seated at the table, waiting for the biscuits and maple syrup. Dawn opened the oven door of the iron stove, removed the brown biscuits and set them on the wooden table. John and Dawn sat down. Catching the eye of his son and then of his wife, John bowed his head to pray. "Lord, bless this food and our home. Amen."

"Are we going to church today?" Dawn asked as she handed John the plate of biscuits, "Or do you have other plans?" she added hopefully. She seldom felt comfortable at the Hazelwood Mission Church, where the other women would stare at her, making clear the utter lack of respect they had for her, a white woman who would marry an Indian. The fact that she dearly loved John was the only reason she put aside her feelings and attended services with him.

John had much respect for the missionaries who had served the small settlement church. They were fluent in the Dakota language, which aided his understanding of the Bible and its teachings.

"Yes, we are going," he replied gently. "I know you are not pleased with the way some of the *Iasecas* — bad mouthers — treat you. But we do have friends there, like our neighbors, the Sinks family. There is much to be learned from the missionary who treats us well, so we should try to forgive, like the Good Book tells us."

They finished their morning meal and then John and Little

Wind went out to harness the horses for the five-mile trip in to the Mission. Dawn went about doing the dishes and dressed for church. After hitching the horses to the wagon, John and Little Wind climbed up on the seat to wait for Dawn.

It crossed John's mind that there was more to worry about than how people looked at them. John was well aware of the unrest of the Dakota Nation. Government annuities established by treaty for the Dakotas usually ended up in the hands of the traders, who claimed that the money was owed them by the Dakotas. Goods from the warehouse were issued sparingly or, as of late, not at all. The Indian agent, Thomas J. Galbraith, didn't want to issue goods until the annuities arrived. The frequent confrontations were building into an explosive situation, and John knew there was going to be big trouble. Warriors who had no means to satisfy their hungry families grew increasingly short-tempered.

Dawn came out of the house and, with a hand from John, climbed up on the seat with her family, giving John a fleeting smile. John gave the horses a slap with the slack of the reins and drove out of the yard onto the familiar trail to the Hazelwood Mission.

John was a little nervous about being away from the farm for more than a few hours. Some other cuthairs who had left their farms unguarded for a short time had come back to find their property ransacked by angry warriors of the Soldiers' Lodge.

Spying a slender broken tree branch in the back of the wagon box, Little Wind clambered over the back of the bench, turning the stick into an imaginary rifle, which he proceeded to train on every potential enemy hiding place in the passing countryside. Up front, John touched the arm of Dawn's proper long-sleeved church dress, a garment much too warm to be comfortable on a humid August day.

"Right after services, we will return home," he said softly.

Dawn smiled at him and returned a bold caress, discreetly hidden from the view of their observant young child. At that moment, Little Wind piped up from his place on the blanket in the wagon box.

"Can I get my pony out and ride when we get home?" he asked.

John turned and shared with his son the warm smile that his wife's affection had generated.

"We will take a ride together, young warrior, and hunt some meat for the table," he replied.

Dawn was happy that the two would be gone for awhile and she would have some time to herself to do some embroidery or maybe take a little nap. It would be a nice, quiet afternoon.

Perhaps if the wind could have whispered to her in words she understood, she would have known that this would be the last quiet afternoon along the Minnesota River for a long time to come.

Services at the mission were not that much different from any other Sunday. The Reverend Stephen R. Riggs preached in his usual way about "loving thy neighbor as thyself." Dawn was hard-pressed to believe that his sermon penetrated beyond the listeners' ears to the heart-targets. Following the service, her persistent attempts to socialize were met with the same frosty glares she had received from the "proper" people on every previous Sunday. It made no difference to them that her husband was a good man of strong character.

Dawn's weekly social snub was blessedly cut short because John, with the help of Little Wind, immediately untied the team of horses from the wagon wheels and hitched them to the wagon. John helped Dawn up onto the seat and Little Wind crawled into the wagon box. The ride home was pleasant as it was a bright sunny day with a slight breeze cooling the air.

It was August 17, and Dawn remembered she would have a birthday in exactly one month. She would have to start dropping little hints to John so he would not forget about it. John wasn't one to keep track of dates. Dawn liked to be remembered on her birthday, as it was a link to her days growing up back East.

Dawn was usually so busy with her home and garden that she rarely had time to pause and reflect on her life before meeting John. She had lost both of her parents in a three-year period before coming West. Her dad had died from a lifetime of swilling booze.

Her mother had given up hope after coping with a drunken husband for so many years. Dawn's love and care had not been enough to sustain her mother, who followed her husband to the grave before long.

There had been little joy in Dawn's life. She worked long hours in the restaurant and then went home, with not much to do but launder her uniform to wear again the next day. Worst of all had been the agony of enduring the suggestive remarks made by the rude men who patronized the restaurant. Being here with John and Little Wind was like heaven in comparison.

So it was with deep pleasure that Dawn served her family, and did all she could to make their simple home a place of peace and contentment. She was rewarded for her efforts with great affection and sincere appreciation, especially for her good cooking. This Sunday's dinner was no different.

Little Wind, John noticed, had been bolting down his food, eager to be finished and away from the table. Going hunting with Little Wind at his side was always something special for John. It was his chance to teach Little Wind the way of the hunter. He rarely had to tell Little Wind something twice.

John caught Dawn's eye and nodded slightly toward Little Wind, who had cleaned the last morsel of food from his plate. His cheeks made him look like a squirrel with a mouth full of nuts. Rising from the table, he told Dawn that he and Little Wind would not range too far from the farm on their hunting trip. They were soon on their horses and out of sight.

Dawn hurried to finish the dishes so that she could begin the things she had planned for the afternoon. She so enjoyed the fine brick home built for them by the government. For a time after they moved into the house she found herself trying to justify living in a home provided by the government. As she became more aware of the injustices endured by the Dakota people at the hands of this same government, she decided it was small payment in return.

John had worked hard to make the home comfortable. Making furniture did not come naturally to John, but Dawn learned soon after marrying him that he could do 'most anything he set his mind and hands to doing. Dawn thought of the comfortable bed he had made for them and her face flushed. He made it strong, he had teased her, to withstand the hard use that it would have to bear.

The afternoon passed swiftly and the father-son hunting team returned with a small deer tied behind John's saddle. They had flushed it out of a coulee where the deer had been lying in some tall grass. John had slipped off his horse to a kneeling position, brought the sights into line on the deer and fired. The deer had dropped in its tracks. John seldom missed with his Henry rifle.

With fewer deer about, one didn't want to miss too often. Food was scarce and John was pleased he could add venison to the garden vegetables Dawn grew. God had provided well for his family, John mused.

Hanging the deer in a tree, John went about skinning it and quartering the carcass. Dawn would cook the meat to keep it from spoiling. He wrapped a hind quarter of the meat in a piece of the hide. After the evening meal they would take it over to his white friend, Noah Sinks, who had a wife and three children to feed. Noah had shared food with him many times.

Dawn dug a few potatoes from the garden to go along with the fresh meat for their evening meal. The potatoes were small and would be much larger by the end of the hot moon. By then they would have sweet corn for the table. John finished taking care of the chores outside and washed up, looking forward to the meal ahead.

Little Wind fed some scraps from the deer to his dog, who had just returned from one of his days away from the farm. Sometimes when he returned he smelled terrible because of an encounter with a skunk. No one wanted to get near enough to pet him until soap and time took away the smell.

Then Little Wind retrieved his stick from the wagon box and practiced sighting his would-be rifle on the antlerless deer-hound, shooting from a kneeling position, of course. The dog-deer dropped in its tracks. Well ... it should have, for he had hit it dead center, just like his father did. With that decided, Little Wind leaned his rifle against the house, washed up, went inside and slid into his chair at the table.

After the dishes were washed and dried John harnessed up the team and the family took the deer meat over to the Sinks house near the agency. When they arrived Noah and his family welcomed them warmly. John and Noah unhitched the team and tied the horses to a wheel. The women took the meat and went into the house to visit while John and Noah stayed outside, seating themselves on the ground by the house. The children ran off to play.

In their visits, John learned much from Noah, who was fluent in the Dakota language. Their friendship had grown over the years and through the countless visits pertaining to agency matters. Noah and Dawn had during the past four years taught John to speak English.

The evening passed quickly as the two men talked.

"Is there any news about the annuity money coming?" John asked.

Noah shook his head, cursing the agency head.

"If Galbraith had his way, it would not be distributed if it did come. He refuses to release what rations are on hand, insisting that it must be handed out with the annuities. He cares not that there are hungry Dakota families living on roots or whatever they can find to eat," Noah said.

"Maybe Galbraith needs to be pushed a little harder," John suggested.

"My pleas to him fall on deaf ears, and if I push him too hard, I may lose my job," Noah explained.

"How about the missionaries?" John asked.

"I don't dare say too much because Galbraith can make it tough for them, too. I don't know what's going to happen," Noah said.

John turned to look Noah in the eyes.

"My friend, the rumblings I hear concerning this matter are bad. Real bad. It will not take much — just some excuse — and the Soldiers' Lodges will hold back no longer, and all the words of those who do not want war will be like little puffs of wind in a storm. The depth of their anger will know no bounds. There will be much killing before it is over."

John stopped to lower his voice, as his eyes turned to where their children were playing happily together.

"Looking into the faces of hungry children can stir the blood of a warrior like nothing else can. They will have their day, when and if it starts," he predicted.

Their eyes followed the children's merry play as they thought of their families and the danger they would be in if war broke out.

"Noah, if the killing starts, there will be a lot of Dakotas who will not want to fight, but in the eyes of the whites, we will all be 'bad Indians.' Everyone will have to choose a path to follow," he said. "I will not kill whites, nor will I kill my brothers of the Dakota Nation unless forced to so do. I have chosen to become a *Jesuswacinyan* — Christian — and in the laws written in the Good Book it says not to kill. My warrior days are past, and I have chosen the white path to follow, wherever it leads. I must do this for my family and myself."

Noah looked into his visitor's eyes as his own slicked over with sudden tears that could not be restrained.

"John, I am proud to call you friend." Noah reached out and took John's hand in his, shaking it firmly and holding it for just the few seconds longer that indicated the depth of their friendship.

John regretfully stood to his feet, putting an end to their weighty conversation.

"We must return home soon, as I do not like to be gone too long," John said. "I would hate to see everything I have worked so hard for burned to the ground. As you know, other cuthairs like myself have lost much."

"Come into the house and we'll have some coffee with the ladies before you leave, " Noah said, giving John a playful slap on the shoulder. "If you do have trouble, send up one of those smoke signals you Indians are famous for, and I'll come a-runnin'."

John saw the smile on Noah's face. If trouble came, John knew he could count on his friend.

Everything appeared as it should be in the farmyard when John pulled the team to a halt near their house. Little Wind bounced out of the back of the wagon and helped Dawn step down. The hint of a smile that crossed John's face was not lost on Little Wind. He felt good all over when he knew he had done something to earn his dad's respect.

"This young warrior and I will put the team away and do the chores, and we will shut the chicken coop door if they are on the roosts," John said to Dawn.

Dawn smiled her appreciation. Given the presence of their too-perceptive young one, Dawn could use only a small rise of one

eyebrow to communicate the deeper meaning to her parting words.
"And I will get ready for bed."

The implication in her voice sent a delicious tremor through John. He was glad it was Sunday, and he was well rested for the night ahead of him.

Little Wind climbed up beside John for the ride to the barn.

"Can I drive?" he asked.

John handed the reins to him without a word. Little Wind took up the slack in the reins, careful to not get them so tight that the horses wouldn't move forward. With a small slap of the reins, he screwed up his lips and did his best to imitate the clucking noise John made to get the horses moving. Reaching forward to give himself more slack, Little Wind snapped the reins to the backs of the horses and was rewarded by their lively steps forward. Again taking up the slack, he drove to where John always parked the wagon.

"Whoa," Little Wind said with authority, trying to sound as much like a man as he could while he pulled back on the reins. The horses came to a standstill and Little Wind looked up out of the corner of his eyes, searching for an expression on John's face. He was rewarded with a smile.

"You drive very well," John said. "You will make a good farm hand as you get older."

Little Wind received John's comment with mixed feelings. Even at his tender age, he already knew that being a "good farmer" was not rated very highly by some of the Dakota.

John unharnessed the horses and put them in the corral. Finding the chickens inside on the roosts, he closed the door and latched it. Dawn's fried chicken was worth any embarrassment he might have felt doing "squaw's work." With the chores done, they walked to the house.

The darkness invading the house was challenged by the candle Dawn had lit. She usually lit two candles for the evening, but as it was near bedtime, she thought the relative dimness of one candle might hurry everyone off to bed.

Little Wind was tired from his busy day. Wanting a drink before bed, Little Wind went over to the bucket of water and drank a dipperful before going to his small room in the corner of the house.

Dawn had begun the habit of tucking him in his bed when the orphan, barely four, came to live with them. Now that he was older John had explained to her that Little Wind was not pleased by it. It was not a practice accepted by young, aspiring warriors. Dawn respected his wishes and now closed his door at night with a soft "good night."

Returning to the main room with a flirting smile, Dawn picked up the candle holder and, without comment, went into the bedroom. John sat in the darkness for awhile, smoking his pipe and allowing Dawn time to turn down the bed and put on her nightgown.

Nightgowns! John chuckled to himself as he knocked out his pipe in the ashtray. It was a practice of a white woman, Dawn had told him, to wear one to bed. It never made much sense to John, as it was soon lying on the floor anyway.

Some habits were hard to break.

Night Visitor

John Otherday stirred in his sleep and suddenly awoke to a low rumbling growl from the dog standing near his bed. John quietly rolled out of bed, trying not to wake his wife, who seemed to be in a deep sleep. After their love-making the night before, they had talked long into the night. There was no reason to wake her.

The training John had received when he was young that prepared him to be a Dakota warrior had never allowed him the luxury of deep sleep. Now, fully awake, he reached down and touched the head of the dog to quiet him. Grabbing a breechcloth, which he quickly tied around his waist, John went into the room which Dawn called the parlor. Tying on a belt that held his hunting knife, he picked up his Henry rifle and slipped out the door with the dog.

As John reached down to hold the dog back from charging off, he felt the hair on the dog bristle. Whoever had been out there was still around. Easing around the side of his brick house, he kept low to the ground and moved cautiously toward the outbuildings. The horses were slowly moving about the corral in an uneasy manner.

A sudden squawk from the little shed where Dawn locked up the chickens at night told him that someone or something was stirring them up. Swiftly he worked his way to the bushes near the shed door.

Before he could challenge whoever was inside, the door slowly opened and out stepped a young Dakota boy. Under each arm he had a chicken, their heads stuck under their wings to keep them quiet.

"Don't move," John ordered in a commanding voice. John stepped out from behind the bushes and the thief stopped in mid-step and froze, slowly lowering his foot to the ground.

Lowering his rifle, John set it up against the wall of the shed, and turned to look into the face of the young boy, now visible in the first light of dawn. John detected more embarrassment than fear in the pint-sized thief.

"Do you need food so bad that you come in the night to steal from another?" John asked. The boy's head sagged a little lower on his chest. It was fair to guess that the boy had been out hunting. With little game to be had, he desperately wanted something to take home.

"How many are there to feed from your cooking pot?" John queried. The boy raised his head enough to look at John.

"*Sakowin* — seven," he answered.

"Are there no other hunters older than you to find food?" John continued.

"*Hiya* — no, sir," was the boy's answer.

"Release the heads of the hens, take them by the feet and hand them to me," ordered John. When the boy did so John reached out and grabbed the chickens by their necks. With a few twists of his wrists, the chicken heads were off and the torsos were flopping around on the ground. In a minute they were still. Small pools of blood formed where they lay.

John reached down and picked up the hens. He asked the boy to follow him as he walked to the cornfield that stood by the garden. As he neared the corn, he handed the chickens to the would-be thief and told him to sit down on the ground to wait for him. He motioned to the dog to stay by the boy.

The corn was not fully ripe yet, but John knew there were enough kernels on the cobs to help fill some empty stomachs. There would be a very good crop of corn this season — unlike last year's crop, which was very small because of the lack of rain.

John picked an armful of ears and went back to the boy to find him scratching the dog behind one of its ears. If Blue liked him well enough to allow that, the boy could not be all bad.

Dropping the corn to the ground, John got down on his knees

and started to weave the husk of one ear to another until they were all fastened together. Rising, he asked the boy to stand, and then coiled the corn around the child's neck and shoulders.

"Do you have a pony nearby?" asked John. The boy motioned over his shoulder, still too embarrassed to speak.

"The next time you are hunting, come by here — but only when the morning sun can smile on your face. Old Blue will welcome you, as will all of us," John said, ending the mostly one-sided conversation.

The boy raised his head far enough to look at John and nod his appreciation. Then he stooped to pick up the chickens and scurried to his pony, which he had hidden in a thicket down in the coulee. John propped the shed door open so the chickens could come out when they wanted to start their daily scavenging.

Ambling toward the corral, John decided to feed the livestock before going back into the house. It was a cool morning, which would later develop into a very hot day. That was to be expected, because it was the Season of the Hot Moon.

After pitching some hay to his four horses, John sat down on a stump by the corral, as it was a little early to wake his wife and son. Blue came up beside John and sat on his haunches, waiting for the pat on the head he usually received. After relishing a couple of pats, Blue left on one of his forays. He probably would not be seen until evening.

For some time now Dawn had been asking John about getting a cow. She admitted she didn't know how to milk one, but promised to learn how. John had flatly stated that he would not do the milking.

John planned to ask around when they got to the agency this afternoon and try to find someone who might have a cow for sale. He had saved what little money he could from working at the agency.

John remembered Dawn saying something about how, with milk and cream regularly available, she could cook with more variety for their table.

"*What a pleasant thought. I'm not sure I deserve such a fine woman as Dawn*," he mused to himself.

Lighting the Powder Keg

Four tired and hungry young Dakota hunters returning from a hunt in the Big Woods of Minnesota moved along the trail that skirted the village of Acton. It was Sunday and the settlers were returning from church to their homes. They paid little attention to the hunters — just as many others had come to ignore the growing complaints of neighbor Dakotas about being cheated out of their treaty money and food rations. Some settlers lended aid; most focused on their own concerns and did not consider it their business if the Dakotas were slowly starving to death.

Killing Ghost looked over his shoulder at his hunting companions who rode slump-shouldered on their tired-out horses — a picture of dejection that went along with being very hungry. Their mood in no way reflected the beautiful summer day that shone around them.

There was a reason for the long faces. The way of life that had existed for so many years had disappeared. No longer were there large herds of buffalo roaming the prairies to provide for the needs of the Dakota.

Mother Earth had been ceded away to the whites by treaties that always cost the Dakotas a part of their heritage. What monies were to be paid to the Dakotas for their land usually ended up in the traders' pockets.

Worst of all was the unspoken condescension the natives read in the face of even the youngest of the invading white people. There were exceptions — whites who were truly kind and respectful to the Dakota. But the others: their every action, every word, even when spoken without hostility always conveyed a single arrogant belief: *"Being white makes me better than you."*

Such arrogance was extremely hard for a proud and noble people to endure. Life for the Dakotas had never been easy, but now it was getting much more difficult.

Anxious now to be away from the village, the four hunters picked up the pace a little. By urging their horses into a slow trot, they would soon be out of sight of the village, traveling south on the Pembina Henderson Trail.

By now Killing Ghost, Brown Wing, Breaking Up and Runs Against Something When Crawling had gone from hungry to ravenous. Their last hot meal was the rabbit they had caught in a snare near the night camp two days ago.

Yesterday all they had found to eat was some not-quite ripe plums and some chokecherries. Three of the braves knew better than to gorge themselves on the sour fruit. Brown Wing learned this the hard way, eating many more than the others. Consequently, he was often off his horse to relieve himself.

Not long after the horses settled down to a walk again the trail wound around some trees and brought the hunters near a clearing. It had been fenced in to provide pasture for a few cows and horses. A log cabin was nestled back against the trees which provided shelter from the winds and shade to keep the cabin cool in the summer.

Breaking Up was the first to spot the hen's eggs in a nest, half-hidden in the brown grass near a fence post. He slid off his pony and laid down his musket to pick up the eggs.

Now we shall have something to eat tonight when we camp," he crowed to the others in exhilaration.

Brown Wing edged closer to Breaking Up, stole a sideways glance at the quiet farmyard and voiced his concern.

"Do you think it is a good idea to take the white man's eggs?" he asked tentatively.

Those words were all that was needed for Breaking Up to explode. Bitterness rose up in his throat as his bottled-up feelings boiled over. He threw the eggs to the ground, splattering bright yellow yolk in an arc, soiling his musket where it lay. Turning to Brown Wing, he spoke with all the venom he could muster.

"You are a coward! Your stomach is growling from hunger and you are afraid to take a few lousy eggs from the white man?" Turning to Killing Ghost, he spat out a taunt. "I did not know we were riding with a coward all this time!"

Being called a coward was more than Brown Wing could take. He slid off his horse. With both hands on his musket he jammed it up against Breaking Up's chest, knocking him to the ground. Standing over him and brandishing his musket, Brown Wing responded in a voice filled with anger.

"I am not afraid of the white man, and to prove it, I am going over there. I will kill him! Are you warrior enough to go with me?" Brown Wing stared his challenge with hot eyes.

Killing Ghost knew the talk was taking a dangerous turn, but he said nothing. He thought the two would come to their senses, given a few moments to cool off. He watched as Breaking Up wiped the egg off his musket with some dried grass and mounted his pony.

Brown Wing turned to Killing Ghost and the others, looked into their eyes and silently waited for a reaction. Killing Ghost responded.

"Are you sure you want to do this?" he asked quietly.

Brown Wing answered by mounting up and loping toward the cabin. Runs Against Something when Crawling did what he always did. He went along with whatever the rest said or did. He was always the follower of others.

Brown Wing took the lead as they turned into the yard and rode toward the cabin. He had said brave things in a fit of anger, and now it was too late to give way to the cold lump in the middle of his stomach. He had never fired his musket at people before. He had only used it to hunt. Now the realization that he would kill or be killed made the distance to the cabin seem so close.

As they rode up to the cabin the door swung open and a man looked out at them. Leaving the door open, he moved back behind the counter of his small store. The Dakotas dismounted and walked inside the cabin to discover they were in a trader's store. There was a doorway to another room partially closed off by a curtain. The faded cloth was thin enough to reveal a girl of about fifteen summers and a young boy sitting beside her on the bed.

Brown Wing, looking around, saw a whiskey keg behind the counter.

"Whiskey," he said, looking evenly at the trader.

"No!" the trader replied as he waved his hands crossways in front of him, a look of defiance in his eyes. It was a word the Dakotas heard often.

Again Brown Wing demanded whiskey, and again the trader said no. Brown Wing bolted around the end of the short counter, followed by the other Dakotas. Pushing the trader aside, Brown Wing picked up a mug and poured himself a drink from the keg. While the others were filling their mugs the trader eased over to the door, grabbed his musket and quickly left. He started down the road a half mile to another cabin, leaving the two children behind.

Having poured their mugs full of whiskey, the Dakotas looked around to discover the trader was gone. Killing Ghost went to the door. In the distance he could see the lone man running very fast to the neighbor's place. Killing Ghost wondered what kind of man would run away and leave his children behind. Disgust welled up in Killing Ghost. In times of trouble for Dakotas, their first concern is the safety of the young and old alike.

Killing Ghost turned back into the cabin to find Breaking Up peering through the curtain at the girl and the young boy in the next room. By now the mugs were about empty. Breaking Up pulled the curtain aside and lunged at the girl, who was cowering on the corner of the bed, trembling uncontrollably.

Killing Ghost raced into the room to find the young boy striking at Breaking Up's leg with fists and feet. As the girl let out a high-pitched scream, Breaking Up grabbed the girl's arm and used his other hand to grab the neckline of her dress, ripping it down to her stomach and exposing her breasts. Just as he began to pull her to himself Killing Ghost grabbed his wrist and jerked him away from the girl.

"Are you so brave that you make war on women and children?" snarled Killing Ghost.

Breaking Up glared at him and the others who had entered the room. Quickly he decided he wouldn't win a fight with Killing Ghost and he raised both hands in submission. He wheeled around and stalked out of the room followed by the others, leaving the boy and girl to cling to each other on the bed, too frightened to move.

Once outside the cabin the marauders mounted their horses and picked up the route the trader had taken to the cabin a short distance away. As they drew closer they could see the store man outside with two other men, two women and a small child.

"Be ready to shoot when I do," Brown Wing said to the others. By now the anger and frustration of the small hunting party was growing, aided by the whiskey.

Riding into the clearing in front of the cabin, Brown Wing raised one hand in a friendly salute, as did his companions.

The settlers faces masked their inner feelings. To them, the Dakotas were like a bad headache that you wished would go away. It was getting so that the Dakotas were more tolerated than feared.

Sliding off their horses, the Dakotas stepped forward to shake hands with the men in a friendly manner. Unable to speak the white man's language, Brown Wing pointed to the well in the yard and to his own open mouth to signify that he was thirsty.

The youngest of the adult settlers quickly stepped over to the well, turned the handle of the windlass, lowered the bucket down into the well and brought up fresh water. He was thinking that the sooner he took care of their needs, the sooner they would leave. So he hoped!

He placed the bucket on the rock curbing, lifted the dipper from its nail on the upright post, and handed the filled dipper to Brown Wing.

Brown Wing noisily finished off the water in the dipper and handed it to Killing Ghost to drink, as did the others. Again Brown Wing stuck out his hand to shake, his friends aping him, and nodded thanks for drink. In reply, the young settler nodded his head.

Turning, Brown Wing handed his musket to Killing Ghost and crossed the few steps over to the cabin. He picked up one of the settler's muskets leaning against the wall. Handing it to the wary young settler, he walked over to a tree and broke off a piece of bark, wedging it back into a small niche in the tree's trunk.

Walking back to the knot of men, he took his musket from Killing Ghost. He turned, took aim and fired at the target. Some bark flew but the target was still sticking in the tree.

Killing Ghost wondered for a moment why Brown Wing missed such an easy shot — and then he knew. Taking his turn, Killing Ghost raised his own musket and sighted down the barrel, pulling just off the target, and scored a clean miss. Killing Ghost stepped back and with a shrug of his shoulders proceeded to reload.

By now it was clear to the other two Dakotas what was happening. Brown Wing wanted the white men to win the shooting match, but also to empty their guns.

Breaking Up raised his weapon, fired and missed, as did Runs Against Something When Crawling. Brown Wing turned to the settlers and pointed to their muskets and then to the target.

The young settler relaxed a little, thinking that all the Dakotas wanted was a shooting contest. He took aim and fired and the target disappeared. Nodding approval, Brown Wing walked to the tree and broke off another piece of bark and wedged it in the tree as he had before. He returned to the firing line and noticed that his friends had reloaded. Brown Wing pointed to the other two settlers, urging them to fire at the target.

As one of them took aim, Brown Wing backed off a couple steps and waited. The settler missed the target and turned to the trader who had not shot, nodding to him that it was his turn to shoot. The last of the white men stepped forward and took aim. The four Dakotas stepped back a bit more and waited for the gun to go off.

The trader fired and the target exploded into nothing. As he turned around to display a smug grin, his face froze instead in an expression of stark terror. The Dakotas now had their muskets aimed at the whites.

Brown Wing shot the storekeeper point blank. Before the first victim crumpled to the ground, Killing Ghost and Breaking Up had fired as well, and the other two settlers fell dead. Runs Against Something When Crawling had only the two women to fire at, and he chose the woman closest to him and pulled the trigger. The woman staggered back a step, fell against the cabin, slid down and rolled over on her back, her vacant eyes staring at the sun.

The woman holding the child backed away screaming, fled

around the corner of the cabin and fell down into the cellar entrance.

The sudden realization of what they had done galvanized the Dakotas into action. Forgetting about the woman and child, they reloaded their guns and sprinted to their horses. Once astride, they wheeled around and out of the yard, going back the way they had come.

Nearing the cabin they had left earlier, the Dakotas were surprised to see the young girl standing frozen in the doorway, able only to scream. She had heard the guns, and knew there must be trouble.

Breaking Up pulled his horse to a stop, took aim at the girl and fired. The screaming stopped short as she collapsed in the doorway. He thought to himself that if he couldn't have her, no one else would. They didn't have time for him to enjoy himself, so it was an easy decision for him to make. What was one more killing going to change?

The violent killing of the settlers had taken only a brief moment in time. The hunters — who had been in trouble before — had no idea of the consequences that would follow. It would serve to fan an already explosive situation into an uprising that would forever change the Dakota way of life.

Killing Ghost decided it was time for someone with a cooler head to take charge if they were going to get away from here and leave for home. At best it would be late when they arrived back at Red Middle Voice's camp where they lived on the reservation near the Redwood Agency.

Turning to the others, he told them to look in the shed near the gate for some rope for the horses in the pasture. He knew the horses they were riding would not carry them all the way home without a rest. Killing Ghost rode up to the gate, dismounted, opened it and waited, sizing up the six horses in the pasture. It was not hard to decide which horses they should take. Two of them were larger horses used to pull the white man's plow. The other four would have to do.

Four Dakotas, riding as fast as they could go, each leading a horse, would draw a lot of attention. They would ride their own horses for awhile, but if they could not avoid riding near the cabins of white people, they would have to switch over to the fresh horses and leave their own behind.

The other three warriors trotted up with ropes. Killing Ghost pulled the gate back, letting the others into the pasture. The horses were quite tame, so it was easy to catch them.

Soon they were at the gate with the four horses. Killing Ghost swung up on his horse and took one of the extras and they all drummed out of the yard, moving down the trail toward the river and their village. The reality of what they had done had a sobering effect on the Dakotas, and they put their heels to their mounts, wanting only to get away from there and to get back to their village.

Dakotas Declare War

It was late at night when the tired hunters crossed the Minnesota River on their stolen horses and rode into the Rice Creek Village. Their noisy arrival woke up the camp dogs, whose barking soon awoke all but the heaviest sleepers. Heads poked out of the lodges, looking for the cause of all the commotion, as the tired riders and horses stopped in front of Chief Red Middle Voice's lodge.

The bravado exhibited earlier in the day by the marauding four had all but vanished. As Brown Wing reluctantly slid off his horse, Chief Red Middle Voice stepped through the opening of his lodge.

Recognizing the four confronting him, he knew that something bad must have happened for them to have come to him in the night. Those four certainly would not bring good news.

Red Middle voice looked at Brown Wing.

"What are you doing in front of my lodge, awakening me in the night?" he demanded.

Haltingly, Brown Wing told what had happened, and in the telling kept his eyes focused on the ground. This was not the first time he had been before his chief, and in trouble. While telling of the shootings, Brown Wing felt a cold chill working its way down his back. Red Middle Voice's eyes seemed to turn cold as steel in anger and disbelief at what he was hearing.

When Brown Wing finished his report, an immediate rumble went through those who had by now gathered around. Red Middle Voice raised his hand for silence and to get everyone's attention.

For a very long moment he looked at the four hunters,

wondering if they realized what trouble the killings would bring to the people. The killing of three white men was trouble in itself, but add to that the killing of two white women and you had big trouble that would surely bring the soldiers looking for revenge.

Red Middle Voice also realized that he and his band of followers were scorned by the other bands of Dakota who lived around the Redwood Agency. It seemed some of his people were always getting into trouble over something. It had gotten so bad that he had taken his followers and moved a short distance out of Shakopee's camp up to where Rice Creek joined the Minnesota River.

Looking at the four hunters, he wished that they would have married into their own Wahpeton band. He snorted with disgust, bringing to attention all those around him.

"What you have done cannot be changed now. The trouble you have brought will not be just our problem, but will cause all Dakotas to suffer. It is not for us alone to decide what to do, so we must go to Shakopee's village and tell him what has happened. We are not in great favor with them, so I have no idea what Shakopee will say or do." Red Middle Voice turned to the four troublemakers. "Maybe Shakopee will want to turn you over to the soldiers!" he said.

The guilty four all looked directly at Red Middle Voice, then one by one dropped their gazes to the ground in submission.

"Killing Ghost," Red Middle Voice commanded, "bring to me my war horse, Swift Wind, and you four will ride beside me." The tone of his voice made the invitation more than a request.

Red Middle Voice went into his lodge while the others were getting ready and instructed his wife to get some dried meat and parched corn for the hunters, as he knew they must be very hungry from their long ride. He also picked up a small bladder of water to go along with the food. It was a temptation to let them fend for themselves, but as long as they were a part of his band he would look to their needs as he would any of the other villagers.

Gathering up his rifle and the food, he stepped outside. He found most everyone mounted up and ready to ride. Killing Ghost had brought Red Middle Voice's horse. The chief handed the food and water to Killing Ghost to share with the others and mounted up, taking his place in front of the warriors. They all started south on the short ride to Shakopee's village, located where the Redwood and Minnesota rivers joined.

The night was swiftly passing away as the warriors raised their horses into a ground-covering gallop on the trail south. Night-scavenging animals near the path of the riders retreated to cover and awaited the passing of those who had interrupted their nightly hunt.

As the warriors pounded down the trail Red Middle Voice could not help but wonder what Shakopee would decide to do. He might want to turn the four killers over to the soldiers, or more likely he would want to call a council of chiefs of the Redwood Agency. If there was talk of war against the whites, Shakopee would be in favor of it. There was no doubt — whatever action would be taken, it would affect all of them.

Nearing Shakopee's camp, the hoofbeats of the unshod horses woke the dogs, who in turn brought the camp to life. It was much larger than Red Middle Voice's, and soon people were stepping out of their lodges, wondering what had interrupted their sleep. Red Middle Voice dismounted and approached Shakopee's lodge, where the short, stout leader stood waiting and wondering about the cause of this late night visit. The quietness of the riders indicated to him that whatever it was, it would not be good news.

Shakopee raised his hand in a half-salute to Red Middle Voice and pointed to the entrance of his lodge, indicating that they should go inside to speak. Once inside, with the flap pulled down, Shakopee asked Red Middle Voice to sit. Shakopee's wife was stirring the hot ashes and adding small sticks that would soon light up the lodge. Red Middle Voice sat down across the fire from the other chief and immediately told Shakopee of the killings that had taken place.

Shakopee was no friend of the whites, and the news sent a shiver of excitement through his body. He knew immediately that now was the time to go to war against the settlers. It was common knowledge that there were few soldiers at the forts because most had been sent far away to where the whites were fighting among themselves. Oh, what pleasure he would find in being chosen war chief, he thought, his mind racing ahead to the inevitable. Yet, he knew he would not be elected. He returned his thoughts to addressing his visitor.

"You and I cannot decide what must happen now, but I think this is a matter to bring before a council. I will send riders to the other camps, asking them to meet us at Little Crow's village," he said.

Shakopee reasoned that Little Crow's village was centrally located along the Minnesota River with three villages above him and some below him. However, the location was not as important as the fact that if there was to be war, Little Crow would most likely be chosen to lead. Red Middle Voice agreed with him. Together they stepped out of the lodge to find the people in excited discussions as they discovered the reason for the visit.

Shakopee sent messengers to the villages of Mankato, Wabasha, Wacouta and Traveling Hail and others asking that they all might meet at Little Crow's village in council. The messengers were instructed to not say any more than they had to say to get them to attend. There would be excitement enough when they had all gathered. Shakopee also sent some of his most trusted warriors to cross the river to be on the lookout for approaching soldiers or settlers. He knew it would take awhile for news of the killings to spread.

Finally, Shakopee ordered that his best war horse be brought up, and he told the rest to get their mounts and weapons. Returning inside, he picked up his rifle, ammunition pouch and war bag.

One of his wives had been busy rummaging in a food bag. She handed him a small skin with parched corn and some dried meat.

As he was preparing to go, he wished once again in his heart that he could be the one to lead his people into war. But he knew, as did the others, that Little Crow would be the one they would all follow into battle.

Ready to ride, Shakopee stepped outside and found his horse waiting for him. He mounted and trotted his horse out of camp, where they all raised their horses into a gallop. The night was swiftly passing. He knew that it would not take long before the settlers would spread the alarm, and if there was to be war, the

Dakotas should strike first. Looking over his shoulder at those riding behind him, he was pleased to see that there were at least ten times ten in numbers.

After fording the Redwood River, it was an easy, short ride to Little Crow's village. As they drew near, Little Six (Shakopee) could see the shadows of the lodges surrounding the house that Little Crow lived in. It always stuck in his craw to see Little Crow live more like a white man than a Dakota. It seemed Little Crow dressed as best suited his needs for the moment.

"He surely must have been wearing the white man's breeches the day he asked for that house," Shakopee thought to himself as he grunted aloud in disgust.

By now the village was stirring from the noise created by the night visitors. Shakopee dismounted and handed his horse over to one of his braves before walking to the door of the house. As he banged on the door he could hear movement inside. The door swung open to reveal Taoyateduta — Little Crow — framed in the doorway.

With a wave of the hand signaling an invitation to enter, Little Crow went back to sit down in the middle of his bed, pulling a blanket up over his legs. As Shakopee entered, he was followed by Red Middle Voice. Little Crow's son, Wowinape, had lit two candles sitting on an upturned keg by the bed. Now a little more awake, Little Crow spoke to Shakopee.

"What brings you and the others to my house so late at night? It is only bad things that happen to make anyone ride at such a time," he said.

Shakopee spoke up to prevent Red Middle Voice from having to retell of the killings. He described how the four hunters from Red Middle Voice's band had killed the five whites at the cabin and trading post, and how his own camp came to learn of it.

"I know," Shakopee said, "the killings will bring great trouble to all of us, so I sent riders to the other chiefs, asking them to come here for an immediate war council. I also sent some warriors out to guard the trail on the other side of the river, and to warn us if anyone approaches."

Little Crow pushed himself back up against the headboard of

his bed. He was already thinking out his strategy for the council that would soon take place. He beckoned to his son.

"Go out and ask Gray Bird to come in here," he said.

Wowinape left the room and soon returned with Little Crow's head warrior. Little Crow instructed him to send in the headmen who were here and to send in the others as they arrived. Then, turning his thoughts to Shakopee and Red Middle Voice, he indicated they should make themselves comfortable, which could only be on the floor as there was no other place to sit. Little Crow then addressed Shakopee.

"You were reckless with words when you sent out criers to the villages to come to a 'war council.' Are not decisions to make war declared first in council?" he snapped in irritation.

"The decision has been made for us," Shakopee retorted. "Now is the time to rid our land of the Wasicuns forever!" He was about to say more when the door opened and other tribal leaders filed into the room.

It had not taken the criers long to deliver the word. Among those who had just arrived were Mankato, followed by Traveling Hail, Wacouta and others whose villages were near that of Little Crow.

When they were all inside Little Crow asked them to seat themselves wherever they could. They did, and remained silent.

Red Middle Voice spoke first, because the ones who had done the killing were from his village. He addressed Traveling Hail, who recently had been elected speaker for the tribes of the Redwood Agency. After telling his story once again, he sat down as a rumble of voices grew in the room. The shock of what they were hearing caused everyone to want to speak at once. Raising his hand, Little Crow slowly brought the noise down to where he could be heard.

"Why are you coming to me?" he asked the group, yet looking pointedly at Shakopee. "Did you not elect a new speaker? Ask him what to do, not me." Little Crow had earlier been defeated by Traveling Hail as speaker for the Redwood Agency.

Shakopee answered his question.

"Everyone in this room knows why we are here in this place, for we all know you alone are the one who is capable of leading us in an all-out war against the whites," he said.

Turning away from Little Crow, Shakopee peered into the eyes of those around him. He spoke again.

"Is there anyone here that thinks the whites will let the killings pass without declaring war on us? Will the agent not again hold back our treaty money as they did when Inkpaduta of the Wahpekutes did those killings?" Shakopee paused a second as he looked around the room at each one present. "I don't think we have any choice but to strike first."

A clamor arose from some of the hot bloods who were members of the Soldiers' Lodge, a group that had a powerful voice in tribal matters.

"*Wokicize kaga! Wokicize kaga!* Make war! Make war!" they cried.

Little Crow just looked at them and shook his head in disgust. Turning to his son, he asked for his war bag. When it was handed to him he pulled out his black war paint, blackened his face, and covered his head as does one in mourning.

A powerfully built warrior with an eagle feather in his hair rose to his feet. Stepping up close to Little Crow, he shook his fist in anger.

"Are you a coward?" he yelled.

The room was suddenly filled with a deafening silence.

Little Crow turned on the bed, swung his feet to the floor, and in one motion rose to his feet, his left hand pulling the cover from his face and his right hand pushing the warrior back from him.

Little Crow slowly looked around the room at those present, and then fastened his eyes again on the insulting warrior.

"Taoyateduta is not a coward, nor is he a fool! When did he run away from his enemies? When did he leave his braves behind him on the warpath and go to his teepee? When did he run away from his enemies? No! Taoyateduta walked behind you on your trail with his face to the Ojibways and covered your backs as a she-bear covers her cubs! Is Taoyateduta without scalps? Look at his war feathers! Behold the scalp-locks of our enemies hanging there for all to see. Do they call him a coward? Taoyateduta is not a coward, and he is not a fool." Little Crow let his shoulders fall in frustration.

"Braves, you are like little children; you know not what you are doing, and you are full of the white man's devil water. You are like the dogs in the Hot Moon when they run and snap at their own shadows. We are only little herds of buffalo left scattered. The great herds that once covered the prairies are no more.

"See! The white men are like the locusts when they fly so thick that the whole sky is like a snowstorm. You may kill one, two, ten; yes, as many as the leaves in the forest yonder, and their brothers will not miss them. Kill ten, and ten times ten will come to kill you. Count your fingers all day long and white men with guns in their hands will come faster than you can count."

Little Crow examined the faces which were turned respectfully toward him, but hard with disagreement.

"Yes," he continued, "they fight among themselves, away off. Do you hear the thunder of their big guns? No. It would take two moons to ride down to where they are fighting, and all the way your path would be among white soldiers as thick as tamaracks in the swamps of the Ojibway. Yes, they fight among themselves, but if you strike at them they will all turn on you and devour you and your women and little children just as the locusts in their time fall on the trees and devour all the leaves in one day."

Even as he spoke the words, he knew he would be unsuccessful in moving their hearts.

He made one last impassioned entreaty, shaking the mourning cloth, still clutched in his fist, for emphasis.

"You are fools! You cannot see the face of your chief; your eyes are full of smoke. You cannot hear his voice; your ears are full of roaring waters. Braves! You are like little children. You are fools! You will die like the rabbits when the hungry wolves hunt them down in the Hard Moon."

Little Crow threw the mourning cloth at the feet of the seated warrior who had earlier challenged him. He stared at him with a mixture of pity and resignation. Little Crow took a long, deep breath and exhaled slowly, pausing for many heartbeats before looking back to the group.

"Taoyateduta is not a coward. He will die with you."

A roar of approval sprung from the throats of the members of the Soldiers' Lodge. They were eager to have Little Crow lead them. Consternation rippled among the others who knew all too well that Little Crow had prophesied rightly a devastating outcome.

Traveling Hail, the elected speaker of the Redwood Agency Dakota, rose to his feet to speak, not only for himself, but for the chiefs who did not want war.

"Brothers," he said, "do not do this bad thing! Not only will the white men come and kill us, but think of what will happen to the women and children, as well as the old ones. When the killing starts, you know the whites will be blind as to who they will shoot. Think about those of our villages who will suffer most of all. Our *hiksiyopa* — the children."

"What difference will it make?" shouted a leader of the Soldiers' Lodge, "Wasicuns have been killed, and we will all suffer because of what has been done."

More shouts of approval followed, and the fever for war spread fast.

"What about the cuthairs?" another member of the Soldiers' Lodge asked, shaking his fists in the air. There was a lot of jealousy and hatred toward them because of the special treatment they had received.

"The cuthairs will join us, or we will kill them too!" Shakopee declared.

Any further argument against going on the warpath would fall on deaf ears, so those who did not want war kept any further thoughts to themselves. With that, the council broke up. No formal declaration of war had been made, but no one had any doubt about what was going to happen.

Traveling Hail, some of his band, and the others who were against going to war gathered together where their horses stood.

"I'm going to the agency to see if some lives can be spared. Surely that is where Little Crow will head first," he said in a low voice to the knot of warriors around him. "Those of mixed blood at the agency will not be safe there. I cannot do this alone, so I would like some of you to go with me."

Members of his own band raised their rifles in answer and stepped forward. Silently they mounted and followed Traveling

Hail. He rode to the west to avoid alerting the war party of his intentions. He would circle around and come into the agency from the south.

Little Crow had mixed feelings about being chosen to lead the war party. On one hand he enjoyed the prestige, but on the other hand he knew it was a losing battle. Little Crow had been to Washington City for treaty meetings four summers ago. While he was there he was shown the arsenals and the firepower that the whites could bring to bear on their enemies. None of this had been lost on Little Crow. He turned to his son of sixteen summers, Wowinape.

"Do not let the war cries and the dancing get your blood hot, as it will do to others," he said gently. "You are my hope for the people in the times to come, when a strong leader will be needed."

Little Crow turned and walked toward the warriors, some of whom had already painted their faces for war. He looked to where the morning sun would emerge and knew that the first false dawn was not far away. There would be no time to waste, because he wanted to hit the agency at first sun.

Retribution

The warriors of the Soldiers' Lodge gathered in a tight circle, describing to each other with heated words the fury they intended to unleash on the hated white settlers. They continued their ranting even as Little Crow approached. He had to raise his rifle above his head to gain their silence before he could tell them of his plans for striking the agency.

Some warriors drifted aside to continue discussing their own special plans for some of the traders and Wasicuns who had cheated the Dakota people and treated them badly. It was time to settle up, and the settlement would be in blood.

Cetan was only half-listening to Little Crow, who was busy giving orders in preparation for war. He had no intention of going with Little Crow. He had his own score to settle. His right hand wrapped around his knife in eager anticipation.

A man of forty-five summers, Cetan had ridden the warrior's path in his youth. As he grew older he had become content to spend more time with Tawiye, his wife. Occasionally he would go on a hunt with his brother and uncle. Game was scarce and often they had come home without meat, yet he refused to become a cuthair and work at farming.

Cetan knew there was no tribal law that said he must follow the others as they prepared for war. He was free to go his own way. From the moment he knew the whites were going to be attacked, he was consumed with the delicious opportunity to exact his own justice against the whites who had hurt him most.

Tawiye and Cetan had found a beautiful, somewhat secluded

campsite in the bend of the Minnesota River. They had both liked the spot so well that they built themselves a summer shelter. It was a place to be away from others.

It was small, with one door. Cetan had helped Tawiye set the poles in the ground for the sides, and he had put in the ridge pole and the lower end pole. Tawiye had done what was considered women's work — cutting bark to cover the sides. Cetan had put up the rafter poles and covered the roof with bark, overlapping the pieces to shed water. Inside they had made two benches for along the sides. One was covered with mats and buffalo robes for sleeping, and the other was where they sat when eating indoors.

In the Season of the New Grass, Cetan and Tawiye had made the first visit to their summer camp. During the ride there, they had decided to build a better fish drying rack. The summer before, they had caught more fish than they could eat, so they had started to dry fish for later consumption.

Upon arrival at their camp, they found that it had been taken over by two Wasicuns, a man and wife about their own ages. Cetan's first instinct was to kill them on the spot, but he knew that would bring a lot of trouble.

Sliding off their horses, Cetan and Tawiye had hurriedly walked up to the two intruders sitting in front of the shelter. With a scowl, the man had motioned them away.

Cetan, filled with rage, had signed by pounding on his chest with his fist and pointing to the shelter. In no uncertain fashion, Cetan claimed the camp. Waving his arm, Cetan had pointed down the river, making it clear he wanted them to leave.

The faces of the intruders filled with anger. The man snatched his rifle, which had been laying beside him, and rose to his feet. Pointing the gun barrel at them, he motioned for them to leave.

Tawiye's face was livid with anger. She fell to her knees and pounded the ground with her fists. Then she pounded her breast as if to say, "This is OUR place!"

The click of the settler's cocked gun had pointedly ended the debate. The issue of ownership would have to be left for another time.

Cetan and Tawiye had left then and went back to their camp,

which was with Mankato's band. They reported the happening to the Indian agent, Thomas Galbraith. Cetan explained to him that their summer home was on reservation land and the whites had no right to be there.

Galbraith said he would look into the matter, but Cetan knew he would do nothing. Galbraith was too filled with himself to be concerned about what had happened to a couple of Indians.

So the matter was dropped but never forgotten by Cetan, who now saw his clear chance for revenge. Cetan would not let the opportunity go by.

Cetan went to where he had left his horse and was soon pounding out of Little Crow's camp. He passed the Redwood Agency buildings as he rode to Mankato's camp. It was but a short ride and before long he dropped off his horse in front of his own teepee where he was met by Tawiye. She had been awakened by the drumming feet of Cetan's horse.

Cetan skipped the greetings and quickly told Tawiye all that had happened at Little Crow's camp, and of his plans for retribution.

"We are going to take a ride to our summer camp and see if those Wasicuns are there. If they are, we will make it for them a resting place for all time," he declared.

Tawiye's eyes glistened at the mention of the summer camp.

"I will get a few things together while you get my pony," Tawiye responded.

A red tinge was beginning to show where the sun would soon come up over the edge of the world. Cetan knew that before the sun fell off the other side of the world, much blood would be seeping into Mother Earth. He knew the anger of the Dakota — how they had been treated so badly for so many moons. That anger would no longer be held inside but would explode into the open in death and destruction.

The Dakota had nothing to lose, as everything important to them, except their very lives, had been taken from them. Cetan's spirits were dampened only by the realization that Dakota blood, too, would be spilled.

The pair had soon passed the camps of Traveling Hail, Wakute and Wabasha. They were headed just beyond Red Leg's camp where they would cross the river. From there it was but a short distance to their camp.

By the time they got to the river crossing, the sun was beginning to take the night chill out of their bones. It did nothing to take the chill out of their hearts. Fording the river at a shallow crossing, they walked the horses into a small ravine and tied them short to some saplings.

Cetan, with his rifle in hand, turned to Tawiye, who was getting something out of the hide bag she had brought along. She turned toward Cetan and revealed the skinning knife she held in her hand. She motioned for him to lead off. She knew not to talk, as the sound might carry.

Both moved quietly, not wanting to be heard as they made their way toward the camp. As they drew closer to the camp, they could detect the faint smell of smoke riding on the soft morning air. Cetan turned to his wife with a look of satisfaction. Someone was at the camp with a fire going.

Easing up behind some brush, Cetan signaled for Tawiye to stay put while he moved forward to get a closer look. With his belly to the ground he slithered forward for a closer look at the campsite. He reached a point where the camp was in full view.

Seated by the fire, the white woman was stirring something in a pan over a small fire. The man was nowhere to be seen. Cetan figured he might be beyond the camp where a small eddy in the river provided good fishing.

Easing back, he returned to Tawiye and hand-signed to her what he had seen. When he had finished, Tawiye signed back that she would take care of the woman. The angry fire in her eyes was a warning to Cetan not to argue with her. Cetan motioned he would kill the man first, and then give Tawiye the go-ahead.

Circling back the way they had come, Cetan worked his way up to the crest of the river bank. Stealthily he made his way, watching for the man who surely was along the river bank. He was careful to stay low and be less apt to be seen.

His quiet patience was soon rewarded when he spotted the man sitting on the riverbank with a fishing pole in his hand, his attention on the small float attached to his fishing line.

Cetan started slowly down the bank, picking his way ever so carefully. He didn't want the man to hear him and turn around. He would have to shoot him then.

Inching his way slowly, he picked the places he wanted to step with great care. He tried to stay close to the larger trees which provided some cover for him. After what seemed like forever, he was within a few paces of the sitting man.

Carefully laying his rifle on the ground, he pulled his knife from the sheath on his belt. He breathed as lightly as he could, and moved forward toward the hated white man. Taking two quick steps, Cetan fell against the man's back. Quickly he placed his left hand over the man's mouth, and in the next motion brought his knife hand around and sliced the man's throat from ear to ear. He let the man fall back. Cetan wanted the man to see who had slit his throat before his eyes closed. The white man's eyes bulged briefly in recognition, then went blank.

Cetan slowly moved along the bank of the river in the direction that would take him back to the camp. He would get close enough to signal Tawiye that he had taken care of the Wasicun.

Cetan would have liked to end the life of the white woman himself, but he thought better of it, knowing how much his wife wanted the pleasure for herself. He had never seen his wife as angry as the time they were chased out of their own camp, and she wanted desperately to have her own revenge.

Usually Tawiye was quite even-tempered. The exception was when he teased her about her ability to noisily pass gas when she had eaten from the bean pot. He would run upwind from her and hold his nose. In a flash, she would take after him.

Closing in on the camp, he gave a hoot like an owl and Tawiye answered in kind. Cetan sank down behind a tree and peeked around from behind it to see his wife walking right into camp up to where the woman sat by the fire. As Tawiye approached with one hand in her pocket, the woman set the pan down away from the flames and rose to her feet. With a scowl she flung out her arm, gesturing for Tawiye to leave. She angrily spewed words that Tawiye didn't understand, although the meaning was clear. In between the angry outbursts the woman shouted for her husband, who could not come to her aid.

Tawiye took slow steps forward until she was almost chin to chin with the woman. A look of hate contorted the face of the white woman. Tawiye's eyes had become almost venomous.

Like a flash, Tawiye's left hand shot out and grabbed the back of the woman's neck, while her right hand brought her knife out of the folds of her skirt. They were so close the white woman didn't see the knife. With a jerk Tawiye pulled the woman the rest of the way to her. With her right hand she buried the knife to the hilt in the woman's stomach.

The woman let out a blood-curdling scream and slumped forward. Tawiye pulled up on the knife at the same time, laying the woman open from her stomach to her breastbone. Stepping back, Tawiye let the woman slide off her knife to the ground.

With a shudder Tawiye turned and walked toward Cetan, dropping the knife to the ground before she got to him. He took her in his arms and held her close. Cetan knew she had never killed anyone before, and probably would never do it again.

After Tawiye quit shaking, Cetan looked into her tear-filled eyes and then let her go. Cetan picked up her knife and led the way back to their horses. They crossed the river and rode toward Mankato's camp.

Hoping to distract Tawiye from what had happened, he rode close to her and threw her a loving grin.

"Come on Thunder-Butt, let's go home!"

Tawiye laughed in spite of herself and picked up the game. As Cetan jabbed his heels into his horse and took off, Tawiye joined in hot pursuit, screaming threats and disputing his manhood. Her tears quickly dried in the new morning sun.

Redwood Agency Attacked

The morning sun was just beginning to rub out the shadows of the night on the breast of Mother Earth. The azure blue of the sky was about to be revealed, for there was not a cloud to hide it. Yet, before the sun would set again a dark cloud, not in the sky, would roll across the land and much blood would be spilled. The lives of the Dakota would be changed forever.

Antoine Joe Campbell knew it was going to be another hot and humid day. He had risen early and left his home, located at the Redwood Agency near the brow of a hill overlooking the Minnesota River. Now he was cooling his heels at Myrick's store, where he worked. He wanted to get on his way to Fort Ridgely to fetch a load of supplies, but he needed to get Myrick's signature on an order to make the pick-up. The upstairs door into Andrew Myrick's bedroom was bolted from the inside, and the boss did not respond to Joe's knock, so Joe returned to the first floor.

James Lynd had already reported for work and was standing, looking out the east doorway, lost in thought. At the counter was Joe's brother, Baptiste Campbell, and behind it was George Washington Divoll, who was considered the local buffoon.

Not being in the mood to talk to any of them, he went on outside. Joe made up his mind that he most likely would have awhile to wait, and he sat down on a upturned box in front of the store. Joe had his drover's whip in his hand, and impatiently began snapping the weeds off their stems in a circle around him, hoping the noise might help to awaken the boss upstairs.

Stirred by the sound of hoofbeats, Joe looked up to see some

Dakota coming. One broke off from the group, and rode up to Joe. It was Gray Bird, Little Crow's war leader. Dismounting, he started to make a war speech. His inflamed voice and his rapid fire speech made him hard to understand. At times he would raise his rifle over his head and shake it to make a point.

Joe understood him to be making a war speech against the Chippewa. It was not just the excited warrior that alarmed Joe, but the number of warriors who had ridden up, and then scattered throughout the village. An ominous feeling came over Joe. When Gray Bird had finished, he mounted his horse and rode toward the warehouse.

Before he could form another thought, he heard two shots inside the store. Baptiste bolted out of the cabin and nearly knocked Joe down.

"Joe! Lynd and Divoll are dead!" he shouted. "They shot 'em dead through the side window! Joe, what's goin' on?" Baptiste grabbed Joe's shoulders and pleaded for an answer from his older brother.

By now more warriors had ridden up and slid from the back of their horses.

"Let's get in the store," Joe said, pushing his brother to the door as he spoke. He knew there were guns inside they could use to defend themselves.

It was too late. By now the warriors were upon them and they grabbed Joe and tried to push his hands around behind his back. Not lacking in courage, Joe crouched and spread his legs to get leverage and tried to throw off his attackers and free his arms.

Joe pushed away from the house as much as he could, thinking that Myrick must be up and could fire from the upstairs window and help him to free himself. Finally, he did break free, only to be confronted by a warrior with a gun aimed at his chest.

Slowly Joe stood straight and looked at the hatred in the eyes of the warrior. Instantly he recognized him as the one who had come to his house one night, very drunk and causing trouble. After waking everyone up with his drunken yelling, he had circled the house, looking in the windows. He had been thrashed for his folly.

"Now I will get my revenge," the Dakota snarled at Joe, who

expected at any second to feel the bite of the bullet. At that terrible moment, he thought of his family.

Suddenly everyone's attention was drawn to a low rumbling sound that was getting louder and louder. Around the bend in the agency road came a small group of riders that pulled up into the yard, bringing their horses to a stop in a swirl of dust. Joe immediately recognized Traveling Hail, who dropped from the saddle and brought his rifle up in front of him to rest upon the hostiles. The seven riders with Traveling Hail were now off their horses and had pointed their guns on the warriors as well, but it didn't take a good counter to know that the newcomers were badly outnumbered by the hostiles.

Traveling Hail didn't give them time to count noses.

"If you fire on my friends, there will be more than two Dakota lying on the ground, and you, Gray Bird, will be one of them!" he announced. Everyone knew Traveling Hail and no one doubted his word.

It was a standoff. The tension at that moment was almost overwhelming. The miracle was that no shots were fired.

"Joe," said Traveling Hail, " we will go to your house."

He motioned the small group down the road. It was an odd sight to see — the two groups slowly walking down the road with guns trained on each other. Joe knew just about how many steps it was to his house, but at this moment it seemed a hundred times further.

As if there were not tension enough, shots could now be heard from different areas of the agency. With all the shooting going on, Joe knew traders and other people of the agency were being killed, and that they were in the middle of an uprising. It would be a blood bath.

While they continued their strange promenade to Joe's house, a clearer understanding of what was beginning to take place dawned in his consciousness. He was well aware that the blanket Indians who lived around the agency were in a state of starvation because they depended on the government's promised food rations and annuities, and it had been a long time since there had been an issue of either one.

As a family man, Joe knew the rage and hatred it would cause good men to have to look into the eyes of their desperately hungry families. Once that rage exploded, its most obvious target would be the unsuspecting local whites who, by the color of their skin and their proximity to the situation, would pay a terrible price for the government's duplicity. Those of mixed blood, like Joe and his family, would be caught right in the middle.

Halfway to his house, Joe caught a glimpse of none other than Little Crow himself charging around a cabin, leading some warriors who were looking for more whites. That confirmed his worst thoughts. Little Crow would not join in on a single raid, but would only be leading a general uprising.

Nearing the top of the hill, both groups saw someone sitting outside by the door. It was Uncle Hypolite (Joe's younger brother Paul) holding a double barrel shotgun across his lap pointing in the general direction of the entourage coming toward him. His sixteen shot rifle was leaning against the wall beside him.

As they got closer, Uncle Hypolite reached back and opened the cabin door with his left hand, never taking his eyes off the hostiles. He dropped the tip of the shotgun slightly and motioned Joe and his group into the house.

One of the raiders stepped forward as if to follow, and the shotgun came back up to point right at his belly button. All of those standing in front of him knew that the double barrel could blow a hole through them big enough to spit through. It was a stand off.

The hostiles had by now formed somewhat of a line in front of Uncle Hypolite with no one wanting to challenge the double barrel in the hand of the determined young man. Triggers were easily pulled, and there was nothing behind which to hide.

In the open frame of the doorway stood Traveling Hail and Joe, who by now had a rifle in his hand. Both kept their guns aimed at the unwelcome company.

Uncle Hypolite looked up and down the line of warriors in front of him with a scathing sneer. While doing so, he kept his shotgun moving back and forth, coming to bear on the bellies of those lined up in front of him.

"What are you brave warriors doing here? Have you come to scare women and children who have the same color skin that you do? I think you should go away before some of you get a bad bellyache!" taunted Hypolite. "My bad temper is beginning to rise, and it would be best for you to go away from this house now!"

None of those in front of him dared to raise their guns to shoot him and invite certain death. With grumbling noises they turned and walked away to join the others. Killing mixed bloods was not a high priority.

Uncle Hypolite did not move until the hostiles had left. Two warriors had remained to watch the cabin, but they stayed back to be sure they were out of the shotgun's range. Before long they left, too, not wanting to be left out of the looting and killing.

When the two guards were gone, many of those hiding inside spilled out into the fresh air, surrounding Uncle Hypolite with cheers, hugs and slaps on the back. They marveled at how he backed off the warriors — a tale which would be told and retold for a long time to come.

Joe's wife, Mary Ann, was soon busy making some fried bread for everyone, as some were hungry and had not eaten anything that morning. Joe looked at his wife with loving eyes that declared how proud he was of her; that, in spite of her fear for her family, she could go about taking care of their needs.

After everyone had something to eat, Joe and Traveling Hail decided they would see if they could move about the Agency without being too closely watched. Calling Baptiste outside, they took a shovel and their rifles and set out for the sleeping quarters of some of the workers to see if they could bury some of the dead.

They were almost to the door when two warriors rode toward them, pointing with their guns and motioning for them to return to the house. It was plainly evident that for the time being it would be better to return to the cabin than to test the will of the raiders.

The hot sun was on its afternoon downward slide but had not gone far before they heard the cry.

"The soldiers are coming!"

Mary Ann and her fourteen-year-old daughter Cecilia ran to the edge of the hill overlooking the river valley. With all the commotion caused by the discovery of the oncoming soldiers, the raiders paid little attention to them. Their joy at the comforting presence of the approaching soldiers quickly turned to horror, as they realized what was about to happen.

Across the river, the unwary troops were passing David Faribault's house, enroute to the ferry below, oblivious to the danger they were in. Mary Ann knew that those soldiers were about to be ambushed, and she could do nothing about it. She grabbed 'Celia's hand and they ran as fast as they could back to the house.

When the cry went up among the raiders about the approaching soldiers, the marauders suspended their looting and killing to head for the river and set up the ambush. Joe and Traveling Hail used the opportunity to find a conveyance on which to load supplies. They had already decided that as soon as it was safe they would get to Traveling Hail's village as quickly as possible.

In front of Andrew Myrick's store stood his own cart with oxen hitched to it. Evidently the raiders had planned to load it full of supplies and food from the store. Traveling Hail quickly untied the oxen from the post and hurried the cart toward Joe's house. Joe had run back to the house to have the things they would take with them brought outside, ready to be loaded. It would be a close call, to escape before the raiders returned.

It didn't take long to load what had been set out, and soon they were on their way. It was about four white man's miles to Traveling Hail's village, Wasuheyayedan.

They were not the first to leave the agency that day. One lone Dakota rider, Susinaki, had left the agency that morning, shortly after the killing had started, and put his horse into a flat out run. His home was at the Yellow Medicine Agency, and he wanted to spread the news of what had happened at the Redwood Agency.

Now, when Joe and his group had covered about half of the distance to the village, the sound of distant gunfire punctuated the air. Without saying a word, the group knew the deadly ambush had been sprung on the soldiers. There had been no way to warn the soldiers, because it would have drawn attention to their own plans for flight. The soldiers were left to fight their own battle.

Before sunset, they arrived at the village. Everyone sprawled out where they could to rest their bone-weary bodies. Soon a few more settlers, mostly women and children, straggled in.

The fact that they had reached Traveling Hail's village did not mean they were free. The raiders had by now taken control of the countryside. There was really nowhere to go, so everyone sat around. Some talked about what might happen next.

Traveling Hail moved about, trying to reassure the newcomers that he would watch over them. Some women of the village handed out food, supplemented by the goods brought from Joe Campbell's home. Blankets were given to those who had none to cover themselves for the night. Sharing was a way of life for the Dakota.

The next morning some of the raiders rode up to Traveling Hail's village with a message from Little Crow. They were to report to his village immediately. There was nothing they could do but obey the order.

Yellow Medicine Agency Apprised

John Otherday's blood bay saddle horse did not especially like being tied behind the wagon as they rumbled down the road toward the Yellow Medicine Agency. After rearing back and jerking its head a few times, the bay finally gave in to the more leisurely pace set by the team pulling the wagon.

The morning sun was just beginning to peek over the horizon and the cool morning air would soon fade away, chased by the sun rays. The freshness of nature around him did little to dispel the black, angry cloud of tension that hung like a pall over the area. Even though there was no one in sight to constitute an immediate threat, John knew all too well how volatile the situation was between the local blanket Indians and agency folks. Nothing was business as usual.

In calmer times, John would have confidently left Dawn and Little Wind to tend to their routines while he traveled about on business. Today they were with him. The thought of leaving them home, unprotected, was unthinkable. He had also brought along the bay because a team of horses couldn't always go where a saddle horse could. It was a part of John's life to be prepared for the unknown.

Looking back into the wagon box, John noticed the bored look on Little Wind's face.

"Hey, young warrior!" John called to him. "How about coming up here and driving for me?"

Little Wind brightened as he bounded over the back of the seat, taking the empty space between John and Dawn. Handing the reins to the boy, John stepped back into the wagon box and busied himself checking his Henry rifle. By leaving the front seat Little Wind would know John was placing trust in him.

John completed his check of the rifle and laid it on the buffalo hide Dawn had put in the wagon before they left home. Grabbing his saddle from the back end of the wagon, he laid it flat toward the front and laid down full length in the box with his head on the saddle seat. Should anything startle the horses he would be close enough to take the reins from Little Wind.

John's thoughts wandered to another recent time of unrest that had nearly ended in an outbreak of war. The blanket Indians had demanded food from the warehouses to feed their hungry families. Galbraith, the agent, did his best to follow protocol and refuse to issue any provisions, but the sheer number of war-painted Dakotas so badly out-numbered the whites that the warehouse superintendent finally gave out pork and flour. For the moment, war had been averted.

Dawn's voice brought John back to the present in an instant.

"There are some riders coming toward us," she said.

John reached over and pulled his rifle up alongside him. Looking over the side of the wagon box, he could see three riders. They were definitely not cuthairs. Their direction of travel would eventually bring them close to the wagon.

"Just hold steady, Little Wind, and do not go any faster. Dawn, be ready to take the reins when I tell you to," John said in a low voice. "I want to see what their intentions are before I let them see me."

It didn't take long before the three riders let out a war whoop, kicked their horses up into a lope, reining them directly toward the wagon. They were bent on putting a scare into the white woman and the young boy sitting beside her.

John got up on his feet with his rifle in hand and stepped to the rear of the wagon and untied his horse. Pulling the horse up alongside the wagon, John jumped on its back and spun him right into the path of the oncoming riders.

The surprise that the woman and child were not alone was one thing, but to have the man riding straight for them was another. The invading trio sharply veered their horses away and were soon raising a cloud of dust behind them. To get into a running fire fight with the rider this close to the agency would be bad medicine.

John returned to the wagon, which Dawn had pulled to a stop. Dropping from his horse, he tied him again to the back of the wagon. John climbed up into the seat, took the reins from Dawn's shaking hands and slapped the reins to get the horses moving again. Looking into Dawn's eyes, he smiled, letting her know that they were now safe.

Little Wind's face showed the pride he felt toward John, who had ridden right into the path of the riders and made them turn tale and run. The man who had adopted him was surely "big medicine."

Smoke was rising from the chimneys of some of the scattered buildings which comprised the agency. John pulled the wagon to a stop near the side door to the main warehouse. It was still early in the day, and few people were about, but John knew that Noah Sinks would be in the warehouse at his work. John stepped to the ground and gave Dawn a hand. Then he engaged his son in light banter as they unhitched the team of horses, removed their bridles, and tied the halter ropes to the side of the wagon.

John was about to speak to his wife when his ears picked up the sound of a horse's hooves at full gallop. Turning his eyes toward the road from the Redwood Agency, John could see a rider coming toward him. For someone to push a horse that fast so early in the morning could only mean that something was terribly wrong. As the horse and rider drew closer, John recognized the rider as his friend, Susinaki. The sweat-drenched horse stopped right in front of John, and Susinaki slid from the horse's back, motioning for John to step away from his family for a private conversation.

"John," Susinaki began in a labored breath, "Little Crow and most of the M'dewakanton have gone on a killing rampage and have killed all the whites at the Redwood Agency. It happened so fast that no one was prepared, or had time to protect themselves. The mixed bloods have been spared only because Traveling Hail rode up about the time the killing started and took them under his protection. He made the threat of death for anyone who would harm the mixed bloods."

Susinaki stopped to catch his breath.

"The warriors are looting the stores and warehouses, and that will keep them busy for most of the day, but when they are done there, they will come this way," he concluded.

As Susinaki sank to the ground to rest, the news sank into John's consciousness. Surprise was not among the thoughts that marched through John's mind. Trouble had been like smoldering embers for a long time. Now it had burst into a consuming fire.

John looked at Susinaki and spoke quietly.

"We must for now keep this quiet until we can get word to Akipa, Little Paul and the others. Will you saddle my horse while I speak to Dawn and Little Wind? Then we will be on our way," John said.

John's family had moved to the side of the warehouse out of earshot. He approached them and tenderly took Dawn's hand in his.

"A terrible thing has happened, and I don't have time to explain now. Stay here by the wagon, and I will return as soon as I can. Do not talk to anyone," he said firmly.

He tightened his grip on Dawn's hand, as if to pass on some of his strength to her. It was hardly needed. She lifted her chin to return John's gaze, along with a brave smile. Even without an explanation, Dawn was well aware of John's concerns, and knew that perhaps his worst fears were coming to pass.

John turned back toward his saddle horse to see Susinaki pulling up on the cinch strap. John untied his horse and slid into the saddle as Susinaki remounted his tired horse. Together, they rode away at a walk to keep from drawing attention to themselves.

It was a short ride from the agency to Chief Akipa's house. Riding into the yard, they found Akipa sharpening a scythe, one of the tools of a cuthair. John dismounted and repeated the news Susinaki had brought to the Yellow Medicine Agency. Akipa's face took on a look of disbelief as John concluded the briefing.

"We must have a council meeting as soon as we can gather everyone together," said Akipa, who was one of the speakers and also respected for his knowledge of diseases and their remedies.

"I will ride out and tell the others to meet at the council ring while you gather your thoughts," offered Susinaki.

"Do that, but do not let the news get to the whites at the agency. We don't want them to panic before we have met in council to decide what to do. We will not have much time to meet before some of the troublemakers will be here from the Redwood Agency," answered Akipa.

"Akipa and I will pick up Inahan on the way, so don't stop there," John added. Susinaki raised his hand in acknowledgment and once again rode away.

Akipa's first steps were in the direction of the corral to get his riding horse. It wasn't long before he was back alongside John, who had mounted. They rode out of the yard to get Inahan, another speaker.

Akipa sadly mused to himself about the imminent disaster just now appearing on the horizon of time. Like John, Akipa knew that bloody conflict was inevitable.

Furthermore, with Little Crow in the lead, it would be no little brush fire, but a flaming disaster. After Traveling Hail had been elected speaker instead of Little Crow, it would greatly appeal to Little Crow to be a leader again — even if he was leading others to sure defeat. He would not refuse to lead them. His pride would not allow that.

As if to escape his morose thoughts, Akipa, accompanied by John, raised his horse into a canter for the remainder of the short ride to the house of Inahan.

If Inahan wondered what brought them to his house so early in the morning, it took only the looks on their faces to let him know that it was not good news. John answered his unasked question.

"Little Crow and a large number of red brothers have killed all the whites at the Redwood Agency, and by now are killing every white in sight. It will only be a matter of time until they get up here to cause trouble for us," John said. "We sent Susinaki to alert other leaders to meet at the council grounds so we can decide what to do about this. We are trying to keep this from the whites at the agency until we have met in council. There is no use in them getting upset yet — not, at least, for the present."

All other plans for the day thrown to the winds of catastrophe, Inahan, too, went for his horse.

"With Little Crow leading them, this is no little puff of wind. It is a terrible storm coming that will probably blow us all away," Inahan declared. Once again, they were on their way.

The sun had climbed half way to straight up by the time they could see the council grounds. There were already many gathered when the trio pulled up and turned their horses over to some of the younger boys who waited to care for the horses during the council.

John Otherday, Akipa and Inahan made their way to the center of the council ring where a few of the leaders were already gathered. They were greeted by Muzzamoni and Inyangmani, the latter of whom was Little Crow's father-in-law.

John noticed three others with their heads together, talking excitedly. Their enthusiasm was self-explanatory when John recognized them as Lean Bear, White Lodge and Blue Face — all Sissetons who would be in favor of war.

Another group was also yelling and posturing. John figured they were Yanktons. As they were without a chief, they would have no say in the council.

Riders continued to arrive, and the group was getting larger by the moment. By now there were more than ten times ten, talking excitedly in small groups.

Another friend of John's, Anawangmani, strode into the center where the chiefs stood. He was greeted warmly. Behind him came Paul Mazakutemani, better known as Little Paul, the elected speaker of the Yellow Medicine Dakota. His face was filled with rage.

Little Paul contained his anger long enough to give a proper greeting to his friend, John, and the chiefs. Then he asked for a quick report on Little Crow and what had transpired so far.

John told Little Paul what he knew, and also mentioned that the whites had not been told, to prevent them from acting rashly until the council had met.

"That was a good decision," Little Paul concurred. "It will take a lot of persuading to keep this group from joining Little Crow — at least those who follow the old ways."

Little Paul looked around at those seated on the ground in the inner circle. Most of the chiefs from the Yellow Medicine Agency were now present, so Little Paul sat down in the place left open to him as the speaker.

"Brothers," Little Paul called, waiting for his audience to focus attention on him. "Most of you have now heard about the terrible news of the killing of the whites at the Redwood Agency. We do not know yet why Little Crow led the attack, and for now that is not important. What we must talk about is where we stand in this matter, because we will soon be a part of it whether we like it or not.

"One thing that should be understood, first of all, is that in a war with the white people, there will never be a victory dance for us. Yes, we can kill white people here and there, but when the soldiers come in great numbers, as they will, the final victory will be theirs."

Little Paul waited for this grave forecast to sink in.

"In the white man's year 1858, a number of us went to Washington City for the treaty meeting. We saw with our own eyes the great and powerful weapons their army can use to defeat us." Little Paul looked around the crowd. "Akipa, you were there to see what I am talking about."

Akipa looked up at Little Paul, who motioned for him to speak.

"What Little Paul said is true. There is something else to consider — the number of soldiers they have to fight with. Their number is like leaves on a tree. They cannot be counted."

White Lodge, one of the blanket chiefs, could not contain himself any longer, and he sprang to his feet. With blazing eyes fixed on Akipa, he shouted.

"We know that many soldiers from here have gone far away to fight their white brothers in a big war. Not long ago, when we had trouble with the whites, while trying to get our rations, we outnumbered the whites badly. I do not think there are enough soldiers to stop us from doing what we want to do. If they are in need of soldiers for their war so badly that they will use Galbraith and those breeds who went with him, they must be short of soldiers."

The humor in that statement was not lost on anyone, for their was an instant rumble of laughter and pounding of hands on legs in agreement. Even the cuthairs could not contain themselves wholly as grins appeared on their faces as well.

Chief Lean Bear raised an arm toward Little Paul to speak as the noise started to quiet down.

"Brothers," he half-shouted to get attention, "I do not think the number of soldiers is so important. The soldiers will come and we will all be bad in their eyes. When they first come to our land we made room for them to live here. It did not take long for them to want more of our land, and with every treaty we marked on, we lost more land. The promises of what we were to get for the land was mostly promises. The money allotments for us were claimed by the traders, saying that we had not paid for the goods and rations we got from them. Now we have many empty bellies among us and the white men do not care. I feel bad to see the little ones hungry. I think we should kill the whites and take what food and blankets and other things that were in the big teepees. What more can they do to us than they have already done?"

The arms of the warriors who were not cuthairs were raised, holding whatever weapon they had brought with them and shouted, "Kill them! Kill them!"

John Otherday rose to his feet and looked around at the louder warriors, waiting for them to quiet down. Then he spoke.

"It will not be hard for you to kill a few whites, but what will happen then?" John said. "It may take some time, but soon the soldiers will come and most of you can run to the plains, away from here. But what about those who have no way to get away? What do they do when the soldiers come?"

Blue Face spoke up to say, "It will make no difference, because it will happen anyway. I say kill them. Kill them!"

John heard some hoof beats and turned to see Judge Givens and Charles Crawford riding up to the council. In the absence of Agent Galbraith, Givens was in charge of the agency. Crawford was along to be his interpreter.

"Ask them what is so important going on to have such a large council," Givens said.

Crawford repeated the question. All Givens got for an answer was a view of the top of a lot of heads. Plainly he was not welcome there. Even the cuthairs resented his coming into the council uninvited. Crawford, knowing there would be no answer, touched Givens on the arm and motioned for them to leave. Once free of the council, they mounted up and rode away, back toward the agency. It didn't take long for the war talk to get going again. Both sides tried to out-talk the other. The longer it went on, the louder it got.

By now the sun was high overhead, peeking down between breaks in the clouds. The approach of riders, bent low over their horses, coming in at a dead gallop, drew the attention of everyone. Nearing the council circle the riders pulled their horses to a stop in a whirl of dust and slid from their ponies. Their war-painted faces left no doubt that they were from the Redwood Agency.

Strutting forward with all the arrogance he could muster, one of the riders announced that many soldiers had come to the Redwood Agency and that they had all been killed. That brought everyone to their feet and there was much shouting and waving of guns. Little Paul motioned for everyone to settle down.

"Where is Little Crow now?" he asked, when he could be heard.

"He and his warriors are out killing all the white people they can find," came the answer.

When the uproar quieted down, one of the Yellow Medicine Agency Wahpetons shouted to get attention.

"I say to you, let's take the white man's goods from them, but let them live. We could let them take their wagons and horses and get away," was the suggestion.

This was in some favor with a lot of the Wahpetons, who nodded in agreement.

This brought Blue Face to his feet.

"My heart has been heavy for so many moons now. When we go to the whites for what is ours by treaty, they look at us like we should get down in front of them on Mother Earth," he said. "It is no different if we meet each other on the trail. If they are brave, they will stay on the trail and make us go around them. So I tell you, I am ready to start killing them and put them on Mother Earth."

Again, there were many shouts of agreement.

John could see the mood of a lot of those present was getting very ugly. He reasoned that there were enough of the cuthairs present to keep a balance against those who wanted war. There would be no clear decision right away, and maybe never.

Having spoken his feelings, John rose and told them he would return. He worked his way through the people and left the council. John went to his horse and pulled up on the cinch strap to tighten it. He stepped into the saddle.

Riding past the council toward the agency, John was aware of three blanket warriors standing, looking at him and shaking their guns in his direction. He looked at them only out of the corner of his eye and rode away from them. He felt a chill go down his backbone. It had been a long time since he had been the target of such open hatred.

He kept his horse to a walk for some distance before raising him into a trot. He didn't want to give those watching him the impression that he was going anywhere special.

Spreading The Word

Once at the agency, John rode down to the river, dismounted, and let his horse drink his fill. Mounting up again, he rode to where he had left his wagon, team and family.

Dawn rushed up to him with alarm on her face.

"John, what is going on?" she asked. "Givens returned from the council and said there were many people there, but that they would tell him nothing."

"Little Wind, you stay out by the horses, and if you see any riders coming, you come inside and tell me right away," John directed tersely.

Little Wind nodded and crawled up on the wagon seat. John led the way to the door of the warehouse, entered and stepped aside for Dawn to enter, and motioned her to a chair.

Once inside, John saw Crawford sitting in a corner. Givens turned from his desk and, seeing John, he motioned Crawford to move closer, in case he didn't understand John's English.

"What is going on out there at the council?" Givens demanded.

John sat down in a nearby chair and addressed Givens.

"Little Crow and most of those at the Redwood Agency have gone on the warpath. They have killed all the whites at the agency. The mixed bloods have been taken to Traveling Hail's camp and are safe for the present," John began. "Susinaki told me this when he rode in this morning. I didn't want to tell anyone here at the agency until I had told Akipa, Little Paul and the other chiefs, so we could meet in council.

"This is no time for panic," John continued. "We tried to keep the Yellow Medicine tribes from following Little Crow on the warpath, but there is much talk of killing the whites by the blanket Indians. They think all Indians will be treated the same in the end."

By now Givens' face had taken on a pasty color as the horror of it all began to sink in.

"Those from this agency are generally against killing," John added, "but Lean Bear, White Lodge and Blue Face want to follow Little Crow. I do not think there will be a clear decision of what path to follow, which will give us time to warn as many people here at the agency as we can."

John rose from his chair and turned to Crawford, who stood much taller than him.

"Your father, Akipa, has spoken strongly against the killings," John said. "Do you follow your father in your thinking?"

"Do you think that I would do otherwise?" Crawford answered somewhat angrily.

"I will need your help to gather people here," John said, looking steadily into Crawford's angry eyes. Then John turned to Givens to continue his plan.

"I think we must try to get to the homes of the whites and also to the traders, and tell them what has happened," John said. "We don't know how much time we have before the council breaks up, so I think it is best to have them come here to the warehouse where we will have more room."

Givens nodded in agreement, not having fully recovered from his initial shock of the news of the uprising.

"There is water and room for some wagons and horses below where they won't be seen. We may have to defend this place with our lives before it is over," John added.

"I think it best if only you, Dawn and I are seen moving about," John continued, addressing Givens. "We must tell them to come here without drawing too much attention to themselves and bring whatever guns and ammunition they have with them. I will go to Noah Sinks first and then to the homes I can reach."

"Crawford, will you go to the traders' stores and the houses close to them and warn them?" John asked. Crawford nodded agreement and left immediately.

"Mr. Givens, could you go downstairs and make room for wagons and teams to get inside?" John directed.

"Yes, but first I will go next door and alert Dr. Wakefield, and then get my family. When I get back I will get busy downstairs."

Nodding to Dawn to follow them, they made their way outside to where Little Wind was still seated on the wagon seat.

"Little Wind, I want you to stay here with the horses and if Noah comes here, you help him to put the team and wagon in the warehouse. Dawn and I are going to tell the people that there is trouble ahead, and we will be sending them here. I know you will be brave and do what you can to help, and I will tell you more when I can," John said, placing his hand on Little Wind's knee and giving it a squeeze to let him know he was counting on him.

John turned to the wagon, grabbing his rifle and bullet pouch.

"John," Dawn asked, "do you really think the killing will start here?"

"I don't know what is going to happen, but we must try to save our friends and get them all together where we have a better chance to defend ourselves," John answered as he led off in the direction of one of the warehouses to find Noah Sinks.

There were not many people moving about the agency. Only one or two could be seen going about their business, and John felt good about that. If a general alarm was given, it would be hard to get people safely to the warehouse.

The clouds were becoming darker with the threat of rain and the darkness matched his feelings that there was great trouble ahead. There was no question in John's mind as to what he must do. His Christian faith and his own conscience told him that he would fight to the end to save his family and his friends. The chances of escaping the slaughter would be small if Little Crow came here with a large number of warriors.

John suspected that Little Crow's warriors had probably split up into smaller raiding parties, each going their own way. It would cut down on the number of warriors who would come to the agency.

Arriving at the warehouse where his friend Noah Sinks worked, John and Dawn entered the door to the office to be greeted by Noah, who was working at the counter.

"From the looks on your faces you have not come here to invite me to dinner," Noah said as he rose in respect to Dawn and to shake hands with John. Noah motioned them toward a bench to be seated.

"Noah, something very bad has happened," John said, interrupting Noah's gestures of hospitality. John briefly told about the killings at the Redwood Agency and that he and Dawn were on their way to warn other families and bring them to the warehouse where they would all be together.

"What can I do after I go and get my family and bring them in to the warehouse?" Noah asked with alarm written all over his face.

"You will be bringing your wagon and team and when you get to the warehouse, put them inside. Would you help Little Wind to get our rig inside, and would you water them first? Dawn and I will try to get more people to the warehouse. It will be hard to make them believe what is happening, but we must try."

John and Dawn left Noah and traveled to the closest home to start the job of convincing people to get to the warehouse for safety. At most doors they were met with disbelief after explaining the seriousness of the situation. The fact that Dawn was white and looking very much afraid seemed to have a great impact on the people and galvanized them into action.

It was mid-afternoon when John and Dawn returned to the warehouse, having made their way from home to home. Entering the warehouse John and Dawn walked into a beehive of activity and much noise. Everyone seemed to be talking at once. John made his way over to where Sinks, Wakefield, Givens and other men were talking. As John walked up to them they made room for him to get close and get into the conversation.

"I really don't think this is going to amount to any more than any of the other disturbances we've had," Wakefield was saying. "The report from the Redwood Agency is probably exaggerated. We need to have more information before we get all excited."

Noah fixed his eyes on John.

"John, you were at the council. What are your feelings?" he asked.

John let his eyes move from face to face as he answered.

"Lean Bear, White Lodge and Blue Face want to kill all the

whites and take the goods in the warehouses, as they say they will be treated just the same as any of Little Crow's raiders. Little Paul and other speakers are talking against killing and want to let the whites escape to safety. I don't think that will happen. I don't think there will be any clear decision made and that is what is giving us time to prepare ourselves for whatever comes. I will go back to the council and see what is being said," John paused.

"You should waste no time in preparing to defend this warehouse. I will get back as soon as I can. I think you should have someone on guard outside to let you know if they see any large group of riders coming," he concluded.

John's listeners all nodded their heads in agreement, except for Dr. Wakefield, who still wasn't convinced.

With that, John left the group and made his way to where Dawn and Little Wind were standing.

"I'm going back out to the council and see what is being said. I will be back as soon as I can," John exclaimed.

Dawn grabbed John's arm. Deep concern was in her eyes.

"John, please be careful out there. I don't want to lose you!" she said.

John gently took her hand.

"I will be back soon," he said.

Little Wind caught John's arm as he turned to leave.

"Red Horse is downstairs inside the big doors, saddled and ready to go," he said.

John smiled at him and went down the steps to the big room.

Once in the saddle, John lifted Red Horse into a ground-covering lope and headed for the council grounds. As he neared the council area the sound of loud, angry voices reached his ears. Things didn't sound much different than when he had left. Ground-tying his horse, John walked over on the fringe of the council and slowly worked his way near Little Paul and sat down.

Little Paul, aware of John's presence, waited until another speaker started talking, and then whispered to John.

"We are losing ground as there are more and more brothers wanting to take up the knife," he said.

As quickly as he could, John related what was going on at the agency, and said he would return and help defend the people in the warehouse.

"Did you get to any of the missionaries?" Little Paul asked.

"No, I didn't want to get that far from the agency," John replied.

Little Paul caught John's arm to get his full attention.

"You are doing a good thing and you must get back to the warehouse while you can. I and others here will get to the missionaries and do what we can to guard them. Go now, while there is still much talk," Little Paul suggested.

John eased his way to the back of the warriors and circled, looking for some of his relatives that he had spotted earlier. Walking up behind two of them, he made his presence known. When they turned to him he backed off a way, and motioned them to him.

"You have heard much argument for and against taking up the knife, and I hope you have talked against it," John said, not waiting for an answer. "Those who take up the knife will surely be run to the ground when the killing is over, as there will be no place to hide. Do you want that to happen to you?"

Both of them looked at John and shook their heads, indicating they would stand by him.

"When this council is over, get two more you can trust and come to the big warehouse. I will be there to meet you. Bring all the bullets you have for your guns, as you may need them," John instructed.

The two said they would be there and John gave them a friendly grip on their shoulders and walked away to his horse. The trip back to the agency seemed very long, as he didn't want to hurry away from the council too fast so as to draw attention to himself.

The warehouse had been built into a hill, with door to both the upper and lower levels. Pulling up to the lower big doors of the warehouse, John found them locked from the inside. He pounded on the door and identified himself. The door was opened for him to enter. John loosened the cinch on his saddle and tied Red Horse to his wagon.

Preparing to Flee

There wasn't much doubt in John's mind that there was going to be big trouble when the council broke. The blanket Indians who wanted to plunder and kill would go find Little Crow and follow him. They would do what they had wanted to do for a long time. Kill. John was hoping that those who had been taught by the missionaries might think twice about following Little Crow.

With all the doubts John had in his mind, he knew it was time for action. Time to set up the defense of the warehouse, organize the people and prepare them for the worst.

Going up the stairs, he could see that most of the whites of the agency were there and that they had already done some planning. The space around the stairwell had barrels and rocks piled up, ready to be hurled down on the enemy.

John found Givens and Sinks huddled with some of the other men and as they approached, they looked at him questioningly.

"What's going on out there, John?" Givens asked.

"Nothing much has changed," John reported. "Those of the Soldiers' Lodge want to raid and kill. Little Paul and the others talk against any killing of the whites. I don't know how much time we have, but we better start preparing right now."

"All of us here will be a part of whatever happens, so maybe we should gather everyone together and decide on a course of action," Noah suggested.

Nelson Givens stepped up on a crate and clapped his hands together to summon everyone's attention.

"Please, all of you. Gather around. We need to talk with you," he called loud enough for everyone to hear. The group of about five dozen stopped whatever they were doing and moved close to Givens. When the group fell silent, Givens addressed the folks.

"Otherday has just come back from the council and says there is still much talk. We don't know how much longer that will go on. Some of us have decided it is time to plan a course of action. As all of you are involved with whatever happens, we want you to be a part of the decision." Givens paused to survey the faces in the crowd.

"Before we talk about the defense of this warehouse, I think it would be well to ask John Otherday to tell us what might be in store for us."

With that, Givens stepped down and motioned for John to step up.

As John stepped to the crate, a low murmur hummed through the group. Their faces plainly said what they were not willing to say aloud — are we so suddenly asked to trust a red brother of the savages who are causing all the trouble?

John's impassive visage hid the hurt question echoing in his heart. Why did they still have doubts about him in their minds when it was he, along with Dawn, who had personally alerted them to flee their homes and come to the warehouse for safety? Most of those in the crowd had known John for many, many moons.

"I have just returned from the council," John began, speaking firmly and just loud enough to be clearly heard. "There is much talk of killing by the Sisseton chiefs Lean Bear, White Lodge and Blue Face. Little Paul and other Christian Indians have spoken against any killing and that is what has been going on all day. When they are through talking is when the true danger begins."

John paused to let his comments sink in.

"I must tell you. If they attack this warehouse we must be ready to fight to the end. They will kill us just as Little Crow has killed others. You, because you are white. Me and my red Christian brothers, because we are cuthairs," he continued, now looking through the crowd for pairs of eyes which might reflect a softening of the hearts beneath them. A slight nod from Noah Sinks gave John encouragement.

"It is a blessing for us that they have no powerful leader here such as Little Crow to lead them for now. If it were so, they would have spent less time talking and moved more quickly to action. But soon they will grow tired of talking. We must be ready if they come to make trouble for us. Let us do it quickly," John urged, as he yielded the crate to Givens again.

Givens nervously wiped his hands on his trousers as he continued to speak.

"No one in this room knows more about what we must do to defend this warehouse than John Otherday does. I say we must ask him for advice and look to him for leadership of our defense," Givens declared.

If Givens was expecting a show of agreement from the crowd, he got little. People looked at each other with non-committal expressions. Noah Sinks, sensing the distrust of his fellow whites, spoke up somewhat harshly.

"I for one would trust John with my life," Noah declared, glaring around the room at his neighbors and friends. "John, tell us. What do we need to do?"

John began to answer from where he stood, wanting to avoid looking down on his white audience. As he started to speak, the guard watching at the window began to shout.

"Indians! There are Indians coming!" he yelled.

Shrill shrieks from the ladies pierced the hot, humid air and clouds of dust rose as the men noisily jostled each other, all trying to get to a window at the same time. Fear was taking a strangle-hold on many of the folks within the warehouse walls.

John pushed his way to a window. Looking out, he recognized the four Dakota as the ones he had asked to come and help guard the warehouse.

"These are the ones I have asked to come and help guard you," John announced loudly. "Mr. Givens, would you go let them in the room below?"

"Listen," John called out, knowing it was best to get the people busy doing something. "We must pile the bales of blankets against the windows and then get water from the cistern in barrels or pails. We also must see how many guns and bullets we have." John motioned to the men who seemed ready to respond to his commands, and they sprang into action. Soon everyone was following his lead, by reason of self-preservation, if nothing else.

John beckoned to Noah, indicating that he should follow John downstairs. As they did so, John heard Givens instruct Charlie Crawford to count weapons and ammunition.

Reaching the lower level, John saw there were four wagons and a carriage waiting, and the horses to pull them, as well as his own mount.

"Noah, let's check these wagons and horses over to make sure they are ready for a fast trip out of here if we get the chance," John suggested. Noah agreed.

"We had better get the wagons and buggy pointed toward the door as much as we can so all we have to do is quickly hitch up the horses," Noah added.

The four Dakota Givens had let in were standing by the big doors. John walked over to them and immediately realized they were poorly armed.

"We will find some better guns for you, but first help us to move these wagons in the direction of the door," John said. Propping their guns against the door, the four pitched into the work alongside Noah and John.

Pushing and pulling, they soon had the wagons moved into place and the horses retied to the wagons.

"Noah, if you could find some leather strips, I think we should tie one into each chain on the tugs of the harnesses, so that once the horses are hitched the chain will not make noise on the trail," John instructed. "The sound of clinking chains carries far."

Hearing steps on the stairs, they turned to find Crawford coming down.

"We do not have many guns, and we are short on bullets," Crawford explained. "There is some lead, but no bullet molds, so the men are busy pounding them out."

John turned to the four Dakota, told one of them to stand guard at the big doors, and led the rest upstairs.

John approached Givens, who was talking with Dr. Wakefield. John waited until Givens turned to him.

"Can you find better guns for these guards who will help protect the building?" John asked. "If we are attacked we will need the best guns we have in the hands of the guards."

Givens nodded agreement and motioned for the guards to follow him. John turned to the doctor.

"Dr. Wakefield, I have heard that your family and Mr. Gleason left early this morning for the Redwood Agency. I hope they didn't get caught on the road," John said kindly.

"I hope so, too," he replied in a voice heavy with emotion.

"Would you help us by putting blankets in the wagons below so there are enough for everyone, should we have to leave here?" John asked. He knew it would help keep Dr. Wakefield busy, with less time to think about his family.

John walked over to a window and looked out at the dark shadows. Full dark would soon be upon them. The thick clouds in the sky would only serve to hasten the night and add to the ominous position they were in.

John said a silent prayer, asking for help to protect the people looking to him for deliverance.

Turning from the window, John saw the guards walking toward him with guns provided by Givens. He was pleased to see that they were shotguns — sure to have a deadly effect in close fighting. John signaled for them to wait there for a bit while he walked over to Dawn and Mrs. Sinks.

"Gather up what food we can take with us if we have to leave in the wagons. Divide it up in two different wagons." John smiled reassuringly at the women. "Get some help to store water in whatever containers you can find and lash them to the sides of the wagons. We will need all the space in the wagons for the people."

Then John motioned for the guards to follow him downstairs. As he descended the stairs, he saw Noah still tying strips of leather to the tug chains. John led the guards to the big doors and stopped.

"We are going to go outside and walk around the building, if we can make it. If you see anyone, don't look right at them, but keep on walking," he cautioned the men.

"If anyone is out there, I don't think they'll be too close, but they may be watching us. We will come back to this door and come inside again to decide our next move," he added.

The faces of the guards betrayed their fear, though they tried to hide it from John, the man they knew as "Ampatutokacha, The Fierce Warrior." He was a cuthair, and wore white men's clothes, but they knew under all that he was a great warrior. They took some comfort in that.

As John was about to lead them outside, Noah, having completed his task, approached John.

"I will guard the door while you are out," he said quietly. "Be careful, John."

John acknowledged Noah's words with a solemn nod and lifted the bar on the door, leading the guards outside. He motioned for them to spread out a little, so that if they were fired on, they would not all be bunched up as one convenient, large target.

John stepped into the lead and moved at a leisurely pace, his eyes ever alert to any movement in his field of vision.

The men made the first corner of the building without seeing anyone, but as John rounded the corner, his eyes took in four Dakota sitting together about a stone's throw away. As they in turn became aware of John and his cohorts, they did not assume a challenging stance. They seemed to just be watching John and the guards as they continued their walk.

At the next corner they saw another bunch of five Dakota, about the same distance away, with yet another bunch further along toward the corner of the building. All were far enough out to not constitute a threat.

John was sure that once they reached the last corner, they would see more Dakota at distance, and his intuition was right. For now, it seemed, they were content to surround the warehouse and keep watch. John and the guards walked up to the big doors, gave a tap, and slipped inside the door. They relaxed visibly as Noah put the heavy bar back in place.

"We have company out there, Noah," John exclaimed. "For now, they're just watching us. Anyone trying to leave here would be fired upon, I think. There will be more coming, I'm sure, before the night is over."

"I guess all we can do is keep an eye on them and be ready to move out if we get the chance," Noah added.

By now the guards had taken up positions at the windows, and they had time with their own thoughts. They had been afraid to tell John "no" when he asked them to come, but they weren't sure they belonged on the inside of the warehouse.

John could hear the noise of the men upstairs pounding out bullets. Noah and John climbed the steps to the upper floor. Once upstairs, John looked around at the people who were not busy at some task. The fear in their eyes told him they were aware of the Dakota who now surrounded the warehouse. John walked up to a group and gave a report in a subdued voice.

"I don't think they plan to attack for now, but they are there to keep us in. No one must try to leave this building. The last thing we need is for someone to give them an excuse to fire on us," John said.

"Maybe some of you can help others with what they are doing. The rest of you, gather up whatever you can find for weapons for those who do not have guns," he suggested.

John turned to Noah and nodded to him to follow him over to where some of the men were talking to Givens.

"Mr. Givens, I think the council meeting is over. Most likely, they just quit talking and the council was over. That means everyone left to go do what they want to do," John said. "As you can see, we have company outside, and I'm sure they are there to keep us from leaving. All we can do now is finish whatever is needed to defend this warehouse. The wagons are ready to go. I think it would be well to assign people to wagons so there will be no delay, should we have a chance to run for it," John said.

"I will make the list up and do the assigning if that will help," Fadden offered. The nods of agreement sent him on his way.

John moved to a window and saw that it was getting very dark, and there were a few sprinkles of rain on the window panes. John mused to himself that this could be a very bad night for all of the people gathered in the warehouse.

His thoughts were broken by the approach of a couple of the wives who carried a tray of crackers and a bucket of water.

"We don't have a lot of food, but we do have quite a few

crackers," one of the women offered. John nodded his thanks and took a drink with the dipper they handed him.

"Thank you, ladies," he said, returning the dipper to the bucket. Then he saw his wife and son walking across the warehouse toward him.

John knew his wife was very frightened, like everyone else, but she tried very hard not to show it. He forgot at times how far she was from what she used to call home. She was a brave woman, and he was very proud of her. John handed the crackers to Little Wind.

"Have you had anything to eat?" he asked the little boy.

"Yes," he answered, trying to hand the crackers back to John, who refused to take them, knowing how hungry young warriors can get. Taking Dawn by the arm and Little Wind by the shoulder, he walked over to a spot free of people and sat down on the floor with his back against the wall. Dawn gathered her skirt around her and sat down beside him. Little Wind munched quietly on the crackers.

"I know we are in great danger, John, but I want you to know that I'm very proud to be your wife. You have been good to me and provided us with a fine home, and I am grateful for that." She paused as she leaned a bit closer to John.

"You are a good man, John Otherday, and I love you," Dawn said as she reached for his hand to squeeze it. John took her hand in answer and then put his head back against the wall and closed his eyes. It had been a long day for him. A short rest would help in the hours to come.

The preparations of the people in the warehouse were slowing down as the necessary tasks were accomplished. The evening wore on. Some people, too nervous to rest, huddled in little groups, wondering what was going to happen. Others sat in subdued silence, in acceptance of their fate.

The sound of guns being fired brought everyone wide awake. John was on his feet immediately, and went to the windows facing the river where the traders' stores were located.

The gun reports seemed to come from that direction. John knew that some traders had refused to leave their stores, thinking that nothing would come of the unrest. They were certainly in trouble now.

Those in the warehouse who had guns were now at the windows, looking out.

"Be careful that you don't outline yourself in a window and make yourself a perfect target," Noah warned. The lantern light would be bright enough to cast shadows.

The sporadic gunfire continued, which meant the trouble was spreading to other traders along the river. At the stores where the gunfire began flames were beginning to light the sky as the buildings burned.

Just then there were two hard raps on the door and a groan.

"Let me in," the voice on the other side gasped.

John sprang to the door, drew his knife and ordered the others to cover the light. He lifted it slowly and opened it part way, trying to see who was there.

"It's me. Garvie!"

John reached out and grabbed the man, already on his knees, rolling him through the door. Someone quickly shut the door and replaced the bar as John helped Garvie to a reclining position on the floor.

Someone turned up the lantern and brought it over by where Garvie was on the floor. Dr. Wakefield was soon pushing his way through the onlookers, asking them to make room for him.

Down on his knees beside Garvie, Dr. Wakefield opened the wounded man's bloody shirt at the waist. Garvie fainted as soon as Dr. Wakefield started to probe around his stomach.

"Looks like the work of a shotgun," the doctor said. "Get a blanket over here on the floor, and someone get my medical kit."

When the blanket arrived, the doctor spread it out beside Garvie and willing hands helped him to move Garvie onto the clean surface.

"I don't want to move him until I check him over more thoroughly," Dr. Wakefield said, more to himself than anyone else.

The more squeamish of the folks turned away as the doctor probed for lead shot.

John decided it was time to check on the guards in the lower room. Grabbing his rifle by the stairway, he disappeared down the stairs. A glance toward the double doors found them to be partially open with the bar thrown back. A quick look around confirmed that the guards were gone along with the guns they had been provided.

Angry bile rose up in John's throat as he pulled the doors shut and threw the bar in place. The guards, not wanting to miss out on the looting, had left to get their share. John returned upstairs, dreading the embarrassment of telling the others that his own hand-picked guards were gone.

Finding Noah and Givens, he told them what he had discovered downstairs.

"Noah, would you come downstairs with me and guard the door while I go outside and see what is happening?" John asked.

In answer, Noah grabbed his gun and followed John down the steps and over to the big doors.

"Be careful out there, John. If you find trouble, yell and I will come a-running."

Easing out the door, John crouched to make himself less of a target. He moved slowly to the corner of the building, and stopped to look around. Nothing moved as far out as he could see, which, unfortunately, was not very far. The damp grass would silence any footsteps if there were someone about.

John worked his way to the next corner and stopped to listen with the same results. What could be heard now was more shooting down along the river. The fire had engulfed the first store, lighting up the area around it. John could see a second trader's store had been put to the torch. The flames licked up the side of the building.

Hurrying, John completed his trip around the warehouse and ducked back into the door which Noah had opened for him.

"I think those who were watching us have all left to get in on the looting of the stores," John said. "I think we should get ready to move away from here when the time is right."

"Soon they will all be so busy looting that they may not see us go," Noah added. "Do you have a plan for which way to travel away from here?"

"I think the best route is to go down to the river crossing by Hawk's Creek and then follow along its bank until we are away from here," John said. "It will soon get light, so I want to keep us to the low country going east. We will have less chance of running into the renegades who are more likely to be moving to and from the Redwood Agency.

John took a last look outside, where more fires were starting up and more shots were fired. Indeed, it was time to get going. John looked to the heavens in silent prayer, asking for help in getting the people to safety.

Heading for Safety

John Otherday's soul, if it could have been seen with the eyes in those moments, would have appeared as a flock of ducks lifting from a pond; first, stirring urgently and pressing forward, then, lifting and soaring in confident purposefulness and order. His lifelong training as a warrior gave him the courage and decisiveness. His faith in Jesus Christ gave him the inner peace and the desire to help those who even now distrusted and disdained him.

As a cuthair with a white wife and an adopted Dakota child, John knew he and his family were in danger along with the others. Certainly the Otherday family's chances for survival would be improved if they traveled alone, light and fast. But John knew that if these whites were going to be saved from certain death, it would require all the courage and leadership ability he possessed. He could not consider leaving them behind to fend for themselves, even if it cost him his own family, his own life.

Safety lay in the east, away from the agency, toward Fort Snelling. John knew the country well. By keeping to the valleys and low country, they might escape detection and attack.

"Noah, get the drivers of these wagons down here to hitch up," John began. "Have some of the others bring Garvie down and put him in the back of Dr. Wakefield's buggy."

Noah headed swiftly up the steps and John quickly went about hitching his team to the wagon. Other team owners immediately followed suit. Dr. Wakefield helped others move the wounded Garvie into the back of his buggy, carefully cushioning him with blankets.

The rest of the people were soon descending the stairway. The dim lamplight revealed fear flickering across their faces. John did his best to reassure them with a friendly nod as he directed them to the wagons. He placed Little Wind and Dawn in his own wagon where he could keep an eye on them, and asked Givens to drive. John planned to ride his horse so he would be free to scout ahead once they were free of the agency — if, in fact, they did get away.

In the process of boarding the wagons and getting settled, the people had begun talking, quietly at first, and then increasingly louder as the tension grew. John knew he needed to get them to quiet down before they left the warehouse. That kind of noise would attract too much attention when it was time to leave.

John checked the wagons and made sure the chains on the tugs were not hanging loose to clink and draw the attention of the renegades. He also gave a cursory check of the water containers to make sure they were secured. John took a few deep breaths as he looked around. Everyone was pretty much settled into the wagons. There was not a lot of room for everyone, but at least no one would be left behind.

Walking to where he could be heard by all, John called for attention.

"We will soon open the doors and leave. You must be very quiet, regardless of what you see outside. They are looting and burning the stores, so there is a chance they may not see us leave. Your very lives may depend on how quietly we get away from here. If the renegades attack us, we must fight to the last, for they will show us no mercy," John said, letting the full impact of his statement fall hard on the already sober audience. "Again, we must be very quiet."

Noah was waiting at the doors as John came forward.

"I crawled out the door and took a quick look around. I didn't see anyone close by," Noah offered. "It seems like a good time to get out of here."

There was no need for further conversation. John untied his saddlehorse and moved forward to open the doors. The night's blackness was washing out to an early morning gray as John peered out a crack in the door. He pushed one door open and was pushing one back when a Dakota stepped out from behind the door. For a brief second John thought his knees would buckle. Instead of a renegade, it was Simon Anawangmani.

"It looks like you're ready to leave, John," Simon said. "We've been busy helping the missionaries into the woods, where they might escape to the fort," he added.

"I'm glad to hear that," John replied. "We're ready to leave, too. Goodbye, and be careful."

Stepping up into his saddle, John motioned for Givens to pull out behind him. John rode down the road toward the river crossing. John was in a hurry to get the wagons behind him moving faster. He decided to keep the same pace until the wagon train dropped over the hill, out of sight of the looting Dakota.

Dropping back, John motioned to Givens to get the wagons moving faster. He waited briefly to make sure the rest of the wagons were keeping pace. Satisfied that all were moving along well, John returned to the front of the small wagon train.

The road down to the Yellow Medicine River leveled just before they entered the water. John directed Givens to slow down the wagon train to a creep as they entered the water to minimize splashing. The less noise they made crossing the river, the better it would be.

Once across the river, they passed the Louis Labelle farm, and were soon into the timber on Hawk Creek. John told Givens to follow the trail along the creek. Returning to the river, John took one last long look around. There was smoke rising from most of the traders' stores. He was relieved that no one was following. If a few renegades had noticed them, they would be reluctant to follow, lest they miss out on some of the spoils of plundering.

With a final glance around, John rode back to the wagons. Taking up the lead again, John rode up the trail in the narrow valley along Hawk Creek. He knew that ahead they would rise up out of the valley to high ground and the open prairie.

When all the wagons were on top, John stopped them to rest the horses. Black clouds of smoke were rising above the flames of the agency. Realizing some of the people in the wagons were watching their homes and property going up in flames, John got the wagons moving again away from the brow of the hill.

John led the wagons southeast. Now that they had made it this far, they needed a safe route away from the carnage they had left behind. In his own mind, John figured going toward Hutchinson was the answer. Most of the renegades were likely to radiate north or south in search of plunder and revenge. Later on, he suspected, they would fan out across the countryside, hitting the settlers wherever they could find them.

The prime targets among the settlers were the Germans, whom the Dakota referred to as the "Bad Mouthers." They had never been friendly with the Dakota, and had treated them horribly. Certainly the Bad Mouthers would be some of the first to feel the wrath of the Dakota.

Scouting ahead a short distance, John found a shallow coulee where he would stop the wagon train. It was time to decide on the path for their escape.

John rode up alongside of his own wagon and spoke to Givens.

"When we reach that low spot ahead, drive around in a circle and we will stop and discuss the direction we should take."

John pulled back so he could see his family, huddled behind Givens with the others. Looking into Dawn's eyes, he could see she was doing fine. John was pleased when he saw Little Wind had his arm wrapped protectively around Dawn's shoulder. John let the corner of his mouth turn up in approval.

Once the wagons were in a circle John rode into the center and dismounted. Everyone got down on the ground to stretch their legs. The men gathered around John.

"We must decide what direction to go from here," John opened the discussion.

Several voices were raised at once until Givens raised his hand for silence.

"One at a time now, please, so we can hear what you say," he suggested. Several pointed out that Fort Ridgely was the closest refuge, and there was no argument about that.

When most had their say, Givens looked at John, whose eyes were riveted on the ground.

"John, where would you lead us?" he prompted.

"I don't think the fort is the best place to go," he said, and a few of the men snorted in disagreement.

"I'm sure by now the fort is most likely surrounded by renegades, and we would have to fight our way into the fort. We must go east to get away from the killing as fast as we can," John continued.

Givens quickly backed up John's assessment.

"John, you have safely led us this far, and I cast my vote with you," he said. Noah spoke up quickly, siding with John, as did many of the others.

Three Germans who had been employed at the agency muttered something about going to the fort. Without families to gather up, the three simply started walking south toward the fort. No one tried to stop them, as they seemed to have made up their mind.

John stepped up into his saddle, and in effect brought the discussion to a halt. The rest climbed back into the wagons and they were soon moving east, following John.

The morning sun was by now shining a warm welcome for the new day. The song birds were beginning to trill and John heard his favorite, the meadowlark, off to high right. The peaceful scene was very different from the one they had so recently left behind.

John rode back to Dr. Wakefield's buggy at the rear. On the way he noticed a cloud bank to the west that promised the possibility of rain before the day was over. Pulling in beside Wakefield, he asked about the condition of Garvie.

"He's holding his own, but this traveling will be very hard on him," Dr. Wakefield replied. "If he were in bed, instead of bouncing around in the back of this buggy, he would do better. He knows we have to keep moving."

"The more distance we put between us and the agency, the better off we will be," John agreed.

As his horse was cantering back up to the first wagon, John's thoughts turned back to the heavy responsibility he had taken on as guide for these people. There remained distrust in the eyes of some, and that hurt John. He shrugged off the ache, because its importance paled in comparison to the priority of getting his family and friends to safety. That was all that mattered.

John kept up a slow but steady pace, keeping the wagons to the lowest terrain. It was important to keep off the skyline as much as possible to avoid being seen.

In a backward glance, John's attention was drawn to the cloud bank which had grown significantly since he last looked. There was little chance they would escape the rain storm that was following them. The rain would make it miserable for everyone, but it might also wash away most of the tracks they had made.

His recent years of farming had trained him to often consider the weather and the impact it might have on his enterprise. Now it mattered not to him whether his crops got a good soak or not, for he would not be harvesting this year.

The small wagon train seemed dwarfed by the vast sea of grass and coulees spread out ahead of them. John knew there was a home or two along their route and he hoped to make camp at one of them for the night. If it stormed, a house would provide some protection for the women and children.

Mid-morning John stopped the wagons near some brush and trees. It would be a good place to rest the horses and let the people go into the brush to care for their needs. After seeing to his own, John rode over to his wagon. Dawn was standing by the team with Little Wind beside her.

"It feels so good to stretch the legs after sitting in the wagon all huddled up," Dawn exclaimed as John dismounted.

"Are you taking good care of your mother?" John asked Little Wind as he placed a hand on the small boy's shoulder. His answer came in the form of a smile and a nodding head.

Taking his water bag from his saddle horn, John offered it to Dawn, who drank and handed it to Little Wind, who took a few swallows. Givens walked up to them and John offered him a drink also. Given accepted, and momentarily returned the water bag to John.

"It looks like we could get some rain, John," Givens said, and then smiled broadly. "Getting wet is a lot easier to deal with than being back there fighting for our lives."

"I think it's time to get going," John said as he stepped into the saddle. "With a storm coming, we need to get some shelter for the night, if we can," John urged.

Raising his arm above his head, he swung it in a circle and then pointed his arm east, signaling it was time to move on. Some of the people chose to walk for awhile, rather than sit in the wagon all crammed together.

Once more out in front, leading the wagons, John scanned the countryside watching for anything moving about. His heightened state of alert brought back memories of his days as a young warrior. Being alert was what kept your hair covering your head, not decorating someone else's belt.

The morning sun was approaching the spot where it would begin its journey back down to fall off the earth. Long before that happened, the sun would disappear, hidden by the ever-darkening clouds.

Cresting one of the steeper knolls, John stopped and waited for the wagons to pass. The trailing buggy was about to pass him when someone let out a ear-splitting scream, quickly followed by a clamor from the wagons. John raced to the front, where the petrified refugees were pointing down into the lowlands way ahead. Whatever it was, the people were very frightened because of it. At first glance, it looked like people waving blankets.

John dug his heels into his horse and charged down the hill, riding to keep hidden as much as he could. As he got closer, he was able to get a clear look at the spectacle ahead of him. At that, he slowed his horse to a trot and relaxed back into the saddle.

The menace ahead of them was only a flock of sandhill cranes, flapping their wings and strutting around in circles. The flock became aware of John's presence and soon the birds were running, getting up speed and lifting into flight.

A smile lifted the corners of John's lips, replacing the worried scowl. He turned and waved for the wagons to move out again. He hoped that kind of luck continued. Had it been some of the renegades, they could have been locked in battle by now.

Waiting for the wagons, John pulled his pipe from his pocket and hung it in the corner of his mouth. Just sucking on it would expend some of his nervous energy. He was well aware of how his heart had begun to beat harder at the prospect of a battle. Some things never changed.

A sudden gust of wind, followed by the first drops of rain announced the arrival of the anticipated deluge. Automatically, John reached back behind him and untied a thin leather hide he used as protection from the rain. It had a hole cut in the center for his head to go through. When it was in place, it would keep him and his weapons reasonably dry.

Riding back along the wagons, John could see that people were already covering up as best they could beneath the blankets that had been put in each wagon. The blankets would soon be soaked, John knew, but at least it would help keep them a little warmer.

The first tentative drops quickly gave way to a torrential rain. Even if there had been a place of shelter, John would have been loathe to stop. Putting miles between the wagon train and the agency's death and destruction was more important. Everyone would survive a rain storm.

The Long Ride

The heavy rainfall had lightened up into a steady drizzle. The leaden clouds gave no indication that the rain would soon be over. They had made one stop for the people to get out of the wagons, stretch their legs and answer nature calls. What little food they had left was untouched so there would be something to eat at the night camp.

Early evening found them approaching a house John had remembered from his earlier travels. On that previous visit, he had stopped there to see if he might water his horse. Two white-haired men waving guns had rudely directed him to stay on his horse. They had made it plain that they didn't want any Indian stopping at their house.

Riding up beside his wagon he spoke to Givens.

"I think it would be best if you go in ahead of the rest of us and tell them we need to camp here for the night. I stopped here before for water, and they didn't like the color of my skin," John said without emotion. "We will watch for your signal to come to the house."

A stern look crossed Givens' face.

"I will go ahead, but follow me shortly. No white person is going to stop us from camping here tonight," he snorted. Givens put the wagon back into motion with a slap of the reins, and started for the house.

Holding back the rest of the wagons, John watched as Givens drove up to the house and stopped. John could see the two who had previously run him off come out of the house. There was much arm waving by Givens and the two white-haired men. It looked more like sign talk than anything else, John mused.

Riding forward, John motioned for the remaining wagons to follow. He stopped beside Givens.

"I think these two are Swedes, and I can't understand a word they say," Givens said. "Let's find out if there is anyone in the wagons who might speak their language. He conferred with the others, and discovered that Mrs. Fadden thought she might be able to make herself understood by the two Swedes.

"They may not know of the uprising, so explain to them why we are here," Givens coached her. "Tell them we will camp here tonight and they can join us when we leave in the morning, if they'd like."

"I'll try my best," Mrs. Fadden replied as she walked toward the two agitated Swedes.

John wasted no time listening to a conversation he could not understand. He suggested to the drivers that they form the wagons into a loose circle for the night. If any renegades did show up the campers would have a chance to defend themselves from behind the wagons.

John drove his own team to the corner of the house, effectively making the house a part of the circle. The others moved their wagons into place. John was unhitching his team when Givens strode up to him.

"Mrs. Fadden was able to make herself understood and she explained to the men why we are here," Givens reported. "No one has been here, so they knew nothing of the uprising. They said we were welcome to stay the night, but they were not sure they would leave their farm to go with us tomorrow." Givens paused. "They might change their mind before morning, once they think it over."

John's only answer was to shrug his shoulders as he finished tying his team to the side of his wagon. John recalled the way the White Hairs had treated him before, and he didn't care if they joined them or not.

"I don't think we have enough food for all of us to eat tonight, John," Givens said, changing the subject.

"The women and children should have the food," John

answered. "The rest of us can fill up on water and take up a hitch in our belts."

"I'm sure the rest of the men will feel the same way," Givens agreed. "If you want to set up the guards for tonight and arrange for the teams to graze, I'll help the ladies gather the food together and parcel it out." Before they parted, they were joined by Noah Sinks and two other men.

"What can we do to help set up camp?" Noah asked his friend John.

"Noah, you and I can see that the horses are grazed and watered. We can also line up the guards for the night." John turned to address the other two men. "It would help if you try to find some dry firewood for a campfire. I think we can chance a fire, as I doubt there will be anyone riding tonight. It will give everyone a chance to warm up and maybe dry out a little."

The rain had all but stopped by the time all the camp duties had been completed. Dr. Wakefield had help moving the wounded Garvie into the house and put him on one of the beds inside. The Swedes were not without compassion for Mr. Garvie. They were able to make Dr. Wakefield understand he should stay beside Garvie for the night.

John joined his family, who had taken shelter under his wagon along with the others. The group prepared for a long cold night by laying down a thin carpet of blankets, and then lying close to each other with blankets on top to help hold in the body heat.

Perhaps there might have been enough room in the house for some of them to stay, but no one wanted to go inside if some stayed outside. They would share the good and bad equally. Some still huddled around the fire, but would in time join the rest under the wagons. The night was spent in fitful sleep, waiting for the morning to come.

Dawn finally broke over the Minnesota prairie. The first rays of sunlight danced on the rain droplets left on the grass. The clear sky would allow the morning sun to warm the people and dry their damp clothes.

John Otherday had aroused the camp early, and they were in the wagons and on their way at first light. Without food to prepare, breakfast was a matter of sipping some water before climbing into the wagons.

John kept the morning sun beaming mostly on his right shoulder. He knew traveling in a northeasterly direction would bring them to Cedar City by night. The settlement there would afford them some safety, if indeed the people had not yet fled. Going east from there would take them to Hutchinson, which was more populated.

Riding back along the wagons which were creaking along the trail, John could readily see the people were still chilled from the long, wet night. The promise of a warm day with sun rising higher as they moved along would warm the people and their spirits.

About mid-morning John could see what looked like a small settlement. Knowing the wagons would follow him, John lifted his horse into a canter.

There were a few houses clustered together in a little grove of trees. As John approached, he scanned the buildings, looking for some sign of life. Nearing the first house, John called out a "hello." Silence was his only answer. Riding around the other building he netted the same results. A few of the doors were ajar, suggesting that the people who had lived there left in a hurry.

The only living things in sight were a few chickens, scratching the ground in search of a tidbit. Behind the houses were gardens that were pretty well stripped. John could see that there were still some potatoes and turnips in the ground.

The wagons had pulled to a stop in the center of the settlement. John quickly rode over to the wagons and raised his hand for attention. Everyone was soon walking toward where John still sat in his saddle. When all were quiet John spoke to them.

"The people who lived here left in a great hurry, and I think we should stay here only long enough to catch what chickens we can and dig some of the potatoes and turnips and take them with us," John instructed. "Look for some cooking pots as well. We must leave here as soon as we can. We will eat tonight in camp."

Everyone seemed to go in a different direction all at once. Some were racing for the outhouses, some went into the gardens to pull and dig up the vegetables. The younger ones were chasing the chickens with varying degrees of success.

Climbing down from his saddle, John was joined by Dawn and Little Wind.

"Are you about dried out after being so wet during the night?" John asked as he put his arms around them.

"I wasn't so sure during the night that I would ever get warm again," Dawn replied. "With the three of us cuddled so close together under one blanket, it helped fight off the chill. It feels so good to soak up the sunlight."

John looked down into Little Wind's eyes.

"How is my young warrior doing? I thought you might enjoy trying to help catch the chickens," John said with a smile. Little Wind drew his shoulders up and answered flatly.

"That is squaw work."

Dawn caught the smirk on John's face, knowing he was probably agreeing with Little Wind. John still had a few of the old ways in his thinking.

"We will be able to eat and sleep when we get to camp tonight," John suggested as he remounted. "Will you help get everyone back into the wagons? We must get moving again. We could still be attacked this far from help."

Riding around, John asked everyone to get back in the wagons so they could be on their way. Givens and Noah Sinks joined in the effort, helping the people store their new-found goods in the wagon. Some had found vegetables and others had chickens tucked under their arms. One man was carrying a good-size kettle that had been left behind by the settlers.

When everyone was back in the wagons, John took the lead and they left the empty buildings behind.

As the afternoon wore on, the terrain was becoming more hilly again. John took advantage of some coulees to keep the wagons off the skyline whenever possible. A significantly larger set of hills on the horizon raised some questions for John as to the easiest route. He decided to canter ahead to explore the terrain. John gained about a mile on the wagon train before dropping down into a small valley. There were bunches of brush scattered about with plum trees and chokecherry bushes blended in. It was a peaceful setting.

Keeping to the right side of the valley, John spotted in the distance a gentle rise which would be the wagon train's way out of this valley. He was about to turn back when suddenly he heard a couple of loud war whoops. Two riders came boiling out of the brush just a couple of stone throws behind him. They were galloping straight for John, obviously renegades looking for scalps.

Anger rose up in John as he pulled his Henry repeater from its saddle scabbard and rode directly toward the renegades. Levering a shell into the chamber, John bent low in the saddle. The riders started to pull up on their horses, a little surprised to be so openly challenged by a single rider they presumed to be an easy kill.

John's battle plan had formed quickly in his mind. Aiming at the chest of the front horse, John fired and watched the horse go down, catapulting the rider off to the ground. John levered in another shell and took aim at the remaining Dakota. There was a whine of a bullet flying too close for comfort, and John fired when his sights settled on the Dakota's chest in front of him.

It looked like a giant hand had swiped the rider off over the back of his horse and he bounced twice before coming to rest on his back. John knew he was dead as he rode by.

John still had to deal with the horseless warrior, so he wheeled about to look for him. He saw him lying flat on the ground with his rifle thrust out in front of him.

Not waiting to become a target, John let out his own war whoop and raced toward the grounded warrior. Two quick shots whistled by John before he fired. John's first shot kicked up dirt in front of the man's face. John fired again. The warrior jerked, twitched, and then laid still, sprawled on his stomach.

Circling back, John rode up to the warrior, watching carefully for a sudden movement from the injured Dakota. John dismounted and worked his foot under the Dakota's chest. With a quick movement, John flipped him over on his back.

The Dakota's eyes opened in slits and the mouth curled into a sneer.

"Cuthair!" he snarled, spitting at John. With a last shiver, the Dakota was still. He was dead.

Gathering up the warrior's rifle, John put it into his own saddle scabbard and remounted. He would leave the other warrior's rifle behind.

John rode back in the direction of the wagons, hoping he could lead them away from the scene of the short battle. He felt sorry that he had to kill the warriors, but he had no choice. Had one or both gotten away, they could have returned with more warriors. Killing two Dakotas was the price he had to pay to save his family and the others.

Approaching the wagons, John took his place in front and rode up an incline that would top out on the high ground. Sooner or later there would be questions about the gunfire, and he would have to explain the extra rifle. For now, he would draw them out on the prairie and then lead them straight to Cedar City.

Other than making short stops for the horses to rest, they had kept moving along. John found a place with some scattered trees and brush and pulled to a stop. Once more nature calls were answered and water was given to the thirsty. He had them back in the wagons, other than those who chose to walk, and they were on the move again.

John's friend Noah had noticed the extra rifle and looked askance as did some of the other men during the stop. John explained what had happened with his voice kept low. He asked them to keep it to themselves, rather than get the more excitable in an uproar.

Near sundown John led the wagons into the settlement of Cedar City. To his surprise these buildings seemed empty. There were no signs of an attack to be seen. John felt a sense of uneasiness as he looked around. Turning in the saddle John told Givens to follow him and he led them down by the lake that bordered Cedar City.

The wagons were once more circled up and everyone was moving about, setting up camp. Dry firewood was soon crackling and the women were busying preparing a meal for the famished travelers. One of the men wielded an axe and cut off the heads of the chickens they had caught at the settlement. Water from a well nearby was put to boil, and the dressed out and cut up chickens were added to the pot. The potatoes and turnips would be added later.

"Tomorrow we should reach Hutchinson by noon," Noah suggested. "Once we are there we should be safe from the Dakota." Givens looked at John questioningly.

"Do you agree, John?" Givens asked.

"We should be safe, but I will feel better when we reach a larger settlement," John answered. Before he could say more, John noticed activity across the water, and pointed to the lake. "We are getting company," he added.

A boat with two men in it was moving toward shore from the island. One of the men in the boat waved, obviously happy to see so many people. Reaching the shoreline, the two men stepped out of the boat and introduced themselves.

"I am Robert Baston, and this is my brother, David," the first said, offering his hand.

Givens stepped forward and shook his hand warmly, setting off a round of introductions and handshakes.

"We had a rider come here this morning on a horse all lathered up," Robert continued. "He told us about the uprising and exchanged his horse for a fresh one. He went east to warn others. We all took refuge on the island, figuring we might be safe there."

In turn, Givens told of his group's flight from the Yellow Medicine Agency and how John had guided them thus far.

It was suggested that the people on the island might want to come ashore for the night, now that there were more people to defend the village. Robert and David Baston agreed and said they would go back to the island and ask the people if they wanted to come ashore. Those on the island were eager to come back to their homes, and soon many boats were moving toward shore.

The people of Cedar City brought out food to add to what had been gathered earlier by the wagon train people. Everyone got something to eat. The camp fires were kept going and guard details were set up for the night.

One of the local people mentioned a farmer nearby who might take in Garvie. Dr. Wakefield had made it clear that Garvie was in too bad a shape to travel anymore. Two people volunteered to stay with him.

About the time everyone was settling in for the night, it began to drizzle again. They took cover as best they could and endured another wet night.

Morning came. The rain had stopped in the early morning hours. Soon the wagon train was on the move again. Late morning found them pulling into Hutchinson. Reaching the city meant great relief for the group of survivors, and as they met up with friends and relatives, or found other options, the members of the wagon train began splitting away in other directions.

The families of Givens, Sinks and Otherday stayed together with the remaining settlers until they reached St. Paul. The balance of the trip was made without incident.

First Attack on New Ulm

Mid-morning found a mass of Dakota closing in on Fort Ridgely. A cloud bank on the western horizon promised rain.

Little Crow, Mankato and Big Eagle, followed by their warriors, came to a stop. They were out of range of gunfire from the fort that was in easy view.

The respective leaders of the war party dropped to the ground in a circle to convene a hasty council.

Before any of the chiefs could speak, one of the more brash of the Soldiers' Lodge blurted out a question.

"Why are you stopping here by the fort? Why do you want to attack the fort when there are stores full of goods in the town of the Iasicas?" he asked. The warrior referred to New Ulm. "Iasicas" meant Bad-Mouthers — the name given to the German people of New Ulm.

Before anyone else could speak, another warrior joined in the protest.

"We know most of the men of the town are away fighting in the South. The people are not well-armed. They will be easy to kill," he added.

Big Eagle raised his hand for silence and spoke loudly so all could hear.

"This fort right here in front of us is also poorly armed and has few soldiers to defend it," he said.

Little Crow bolstered the argument.

"If we take this for now, we can attack New Ulm next and take back our land clear to the Big River," he said, referring to the territory on either side of the Minnesota River between New Ulm and the Mississippi.

"I say we attack the Bad Mouthers," spat out another leader. "There are a lot of young squaws there for the taking." This prompted an uproar from mostly the young warriors.

There were speakers for both sides. The final decision was made by members of the Soldiers' Lodge. That was the way things were done.

Warriors broke away from the main body until there were about one hundred of them moving south. There were no chiefs or leaders among them. Their exit was punctuated by an occasional war whoop and the drumming of horses' feet.

"Fools!" Little Crow said, half to himself. "They care more for goods and what is under their breech cloths than getting our land back."

Mounting his war pony, Little Crow headed back toward the agency with the rest following him.

Behind them, activity in Fort Ridgely came to a standstill. They came out of buildings, all casting their eyes toward the Dakota who were riding away. With the few soldiers and fighting men in the fort, they knew they had been staring death in the face. The enemy had outnumbered them badly. Why would they leave when they could so easily overwhelm the fort?

Gray skies overshadowed the Dakota all the way from Fort Ridgely to the outskirts of New Ulm. The settlement was located on the banks of the Minnesota River. The ground was terraced, rising in two long levels until it reached a tree-lined bluff at the top. A slough ran along the rear of the second level, just below the bluff.

The war-painted Dakota, numbering ten times ten, rode along the top of the bluff until they were about even with the houses below. Dismounting, they secured their horses back far enough to be out of the line of fire.

The war party spread out along the rim of the bluff and looked down on the settlement. It was obvious the people who lived below were expecting trouble. There were barricades set up around the main part of the town. The few houses outside of the barricade would be easy prey.

There was no war chief among the attackers, nor was one needed, they thought. Bad Knife took it upon himself to raise his arm and point toward the houses below. A battle cry broke from his lips as he started the downhill run to the slough below. The rest of the warriors let out blood-chilling war whoops and followed the self-appointed leader.

The warriors made their way through the tall reeds and marsh grass that formed the slough. Gaining the edge of the reeds, they had a clear view of the town below.

Heads appeared here and there behind the barrels and crates that serves as barricades. At the first shots from the warriors the heads disappeared from sight. The battle settled down to sporadic fire from both sides. The defenders of the town kept up enough fire to discourage an all-out assault.

Slowly, a few of the Dakota, using any cover they could find, worked their way closer to the Bad Mouthers. Firing from the edge of the slough was a little too far away for accuracy.

To the surprise of the townspeople, a young girl sprang from the door of a house which was part of the defended perimeter. The young teenager was intent on reaching another house outside of the protected area. Halfway across the open ground she suddenly crumpled to the ground and laid still. A bullet from one of the front-line Dakota had brought her down. No one from within the barricades took a chance on running out to bring the girl inside the barricade. At least, not right away.

A fresh volley of fire came from the townsmen as a group of them broke from cover and ran to a house outside the defensive wall. Once inside they knocked out a window and laid down a field of fire that soon had the warriors scurrying back to the slough.

For some time there was just enough fire from both sides to create a stalemate. It was evident that the town was better-prepared than the Dakota had thought they would be.

The dark clouds that had followed them were now overhead and drops of rain began to fall. The low rumbling of thunder grew to loud crashes, with lightning crackling here and there.

The rain was very discouraging to the warriors, but not as much as the group of riders the warriors saw riding into the far side of town. It didn't take long for the newcomers to join in on the fighting. They could be seen darting from one position to another to support the townsmen.

Bad Knife could see that there would be no ransacking of the stores or grabbing white squaws for their pleasure. The rain, now coming down hard, was discouraging as well.

The Dakota held their position for some time, firing sporadically to let the town know they were still there.

Little Crow had been right, Bad Knife conceded to himself. With all the warriors banded together, they would have taken the town in front of him. He now also knew that if they had attacked the fort this morning, they would most likely have overrun the fort.

Letting out a loud yell, Bad Knife signaled for the rest to follow him back up to the top of the bluff. The retreat silenced the guns from the settlement. They didn't have ammunition to waste on targets that were out of range.

Bad Knife gathered with the rest around their horses. The rain was still coming down hard and everyone was soaked to the skin. The scowls on the faces had little to do with being wet. Failing to capture the town and what they thought would be theirs was a bitter pill to swallow.

"Maybe we should go back and join Little Crow," grumbled Bad Knife. The rest didn't bother to answer, but mounted their horses and rode west.

The rain showed no sign of letting up. The warriors were strung out on the road, moving along at a good pace. They were anxious to get back to the agency and under some cover. The taunts and derision they would receive for going their own way was certain to be severe. Still, they had the right as warriors of the Soldiers' Lodge to make decisions of their own.

The thunder of hoof beats jerked Bad Knife out of his smoldering thoughts. The warriors in front of him were doubling back toward him at a full gallop. Pulling to a stop, one of the riders shouted.

"There are some Iasicas coming down the road toward us in wagons and on horses. Let's set up an ambush for them. Hurry and get under cover. They are coming very fast."

The road was soon bare of warriors, each looking for a place to hide his horse. The trees and brush on the north of the road made ample cover. In a short time they were finding cover along the road from which to fire.

The warriors could hear the creaking wagons and horses hooves just before the travelers rounded the last bend in the road. The wagons and riders were coming like the devil was right behind them.

None of the warriors fired until the wagons were close enough that they could not veer away. Then the warriors fired.

There were screams and yells from those who survived the first onslaught of fire. All the horsemen had been swept from their saddles at the first barrage. In the wild melee that followed, the wagons had come to a near stop. The lead wagon had managed to continue along the path with its driver still on the wagon seat. The drivers of the other two wagons quickly jerked the king pins, freeing the teams from the wagons. They vaulted onto the horses and kicked them into a gallop in an effort to catch up to the lead wagon in front of them.

In minutes the settlers heard only desultory fire from behind them. In fear that they might be chased, they kept whipping their horses at a frenzied pace. They knew they were close to New Ulm and safety, they hoped.

The driver of the lead wagon looked behind him for the first time to see only two people in the wagon with him. Counting the men astride the teams, it meant that only five out of sixteen had survived the attack. His own wife had been shot and he had seen her fall over the side of the wagon before he could grab her.

The Dakota went about the fallen whites, taking scalps and slitting the throats of any who showed signs of life. They gathered the guns and horses of the dead and then climbed on their own mounts. Once they were all astride their horses, they started again for the agency. A rider with a smile on his face rode up beside Bad Knife.

"We killed more Wasicuns here than we did at the town," he said gleefully.

Indeed, Bad Knife thought to himself. They did do that, but it was little compensation for their failure to accomplish what they had set out to do.

It was still going to be a long ride to the agency, where they would meet with much shame for the failure in their attack on New Ulm.

Fort Ridgely Attacked

As light crept into the new day, the warriors at the agency gathered around fires, absorbing heat into their chilled bodies. Yesterday afternoon's rain had soaked them thoroughly, pushing the cold deep into their bones as they returned from attacking New Ulm. While the fires were warming their bodies, there was nothing to dispel the humiliation that hung heavy on the defeated braves.

The warriors who had insisted on attacking New Ulm instead of Fort Ridgely were paying dearly in lost honor for their stubborn resistance to leadership. As they tried to restore comfort to their bodies, their spirits were stung by the smirks and jibes of those who had not gone their own way against the wishes of their leaders.

Little Crow, Mankato, Big Eagle, Gray Bird, Medicine Bottle and Little Six had gathered at one campfire.

"Those who spoke with thunder yesterday are rather quiet today," Little Crow said with an expression that betrayed his amusement. "Maybe they will listen better today."

Glancing at the others, Little Crow noticed the other leaders were finding it equally difficult to restrain broad grins.

"Today we will attack the fort and destroy it once and for all," Little Crow declared. "Once the fort is ours, we can work our way east, taking New Ulm and everything beyond."

"I will ride with you against the Iasecas," Mankato offered. Big Eagle nodded, showing that he would join them.

Little Six and Medicine Bottle had no great love for Little Crow, so their stoic faces showed nothing; that they remained at the fire meant they would fight.

"Gray Bird, ride and tell everyone we go to attack the fort," Little Crow requested. "If you carry the message, instead of the camp crier, it will have more meaning."

Gray Bird hurried away to do as he was asked. As Little Crow's head warrior and best friend, he obeyed whatever the order.

The agency came to life as they prepared to leave for the attack. The warriors applied war paint to the ponies as well as to their own faces and bodies, occasionally spicing the air with war cries in anticipation of the battle to come. Even the war ponies picked up on the preparation, dancing and side-stepping about as the eager warriors mounted up.

Little Crow led the war party out of the agency. A backward glance told Little Crow he had about four hundred warriors, most of them followers of Mankato, Big Eagle and himself.

Little Crow was pleased the other chiefs had deferred to him to lead the war party. Considering Mankato's sizable reputation as a war leader, Little Crow was doubly pleased.

Father Sun was still climbing when Little Crow led the war party close to Fort Ridgely, yet still out of sight. It was time to finalize the plan of attack.

Just a short distance from the fort was Little Crow's village, so the leader knew the post intimately. The ride had given him time to plan the attack. The chiefs and Gray Bird gathered close to Little Crow, who shared his plan.

"We must hit this fort from three sides so that the soldiers must divide their fire on us," Little Crow announced. "Mankato, Medicine Bottle — will you circle around to the south and come in on the fort from the east side? Hold your fire until we fire three quick shots to signal the attack. Little Six, will you spread your warriors along the ravine on the south and work in as close as you can in the tall grass?"

In answer, Little Six and his warriors moved out to take up their positions. By attacking from three sides, Little Crow hoped to see where there might be a weakness in the defense of the fort. If there were such a spot, he would send Gray Bird to exploit it. Little Crow kept his own warriors with him to hold his position on the southwest side of the fort.

Mankato raised his rifle above his head to rally his warriors and those of Medicine Bottle. They moved south to circle into position on the east side, where they would work their way around through the ravines and get into position to strike.

"Gray Bird, spread our warriors along this ridge and move them in through the tall grass to a good firing position," Little Crow instructed. "When I fire the first shot, you and another fire quickly to signal the attack."

Little Crow settled back to watch his warriors crawl through the grass toward the fort. While the tall grass was very good cover, the warriors would have to rise up to shoot, making themselves visible to the enemy. Someone decided to steal Little Crow's thunder and fired first.

There was a clamor of activity at the fort. Little Crow heard the bugler calling the soldiers to action. Soon the soldiers were forming up on the parade ground. Little Crow could see and hear a soldier giving orders to his men. The soldiers in the front row were kneeling and those behind them were standing, ready to fire.

Gray Bird and his warriors opened up on the ranks of soldiers. Immediately two soldiers pitched forward to the ground. This brought a louder chorus of shouts from the warriors.

Little Crow saw the leader of the soldiers lift his sword to the sky and shout a command. The soldiers broke from the ranks and took cover wherever they could and returned fire on the Dakota.

Mankato and Medicine Bottle, along with their warriors, opened fire from the east side of the fort, giving the soldiers a new field of fire with which to contend. Quickly, they ran to the outer buildings to use them as protection. Soon they were returning fire.

Little Crow could see some soldiers pushing a big gun on wheels. They moved it toward the northwest corner of the fort.

On his trip to Washington City, the Wasicuns made sure Little Crow got a good look at the Great Father's massive collection of weapons. The show of power in war was not lost on Little Crow. He knew that the incredible arsenal and the sheer number of whites living in the land to the east meant the beginning of the end for the red nation.

Little Crow kept his attention on the big gun and watched them turn it toward him and his warriors. Little Crow's warriors attempted to fire toward the soldiers behind the big gun, but without effect.

Moments later an earth-shaking "boom" was followed by a high-pitched screech and then a deafening blast. The cannonball launched by the soldiers had exploded and rained havoc down on the warriors. No longer were the warriors maintaining their war cry. This was something they had never before experienced in battle.

Gray Bird was as shocked as the rest of the warriors, but he shouted to the rest to start firing again. The stunned warriors were slow to react but finally complied.

Ka-boom! Another cannonball screamed overhead. This time the warriors rose from the ground and ran in full retreat.

Little Crow rode quickly to head off the retreat and lead his frightened warriors into a ravine out of the line of fire. He directed Gray Bird to spread the warriors out along the edge of the ravine. He knew the warriors would be reluctant to charge the fort with the big gun firing at them. The soldiers kept firing often enough to keep the attackers at bay.

Meanwhile, Mankato watched the battle from his location, trying to judge the effectiveness of his warriors' fire. He had watched the retreat on the west side of the fort when the big gun was fired. Now he could see a big gun being wheeled out on the northeast corner of the parade ground. The soldiers were aiming it in his general direction.

It wasn't long before the gun belched fire and the shell screamed overhead, exploding behind him. Mankato fired, urging his warriors to do likewise. In short order there was another big boom, followed so closely by another that he knew two big guns were concentrating on them. The last salvo felled four of Mankato's warriors. The soldiers were laying down so much fire with their rifles that Mankato ordered his warriors to fall back to the ravine behind them. From there they could fire as targets presented themselves.

Leaving one of his head warriors in charge, Mankato retraced the path around to the south of the fort. Soon he was conferring with Little Crow and Big Eagle, squatting down out of the line of fire. Their faces were painted thickly with dismay.

"How do we fight against those rotten balls that break apart and hurt us?" Big Eagle exclaimed.

"We need more warriors so we can surround them and hit them hard," Little Crow answered. "They have more soldiers than we thought."

Mankato left the two men and crawled forward as the firing from the warriors picked up in intensity. Rising high enough, he could see soldiers running for a building some distance from the main fort. About the same time some more of the rotten balls exploded overhead, forcing everyone to hug Mother Earth. The soldiers were soon scurrying back into the stone building of the fort with arms full of something.

"*They must have supplies and shells in there,*" Mankato thought to himself. "*There is no way we can stop them.*"

Crawling back down out of the line of fire, Mankato joined the other chiefs. Mankato told them what he had seen.

"We might as well keep up the attack until dark and then return to the agency. We need to come back with more warriors," Little Crow said.

"At dark I will bring my warriors to join you and we will leave together," Mankato added.

"Have the wounded brought here and we will send them back early with an escort," Big Eagle suggested.

Little Crow nodded in approval. Big Eagle was always one to be concerned about the well-being of his brothers. He was not a warrior at heart.

Then Little Crow's attention was drawn to the sky, which was filling with dark, ugly clouds. Sometimes clouds that looked like these carried winds that tore up the ground and everything in their path. Little Crow knew a deluge was imminent.

The attack dwindled away into sniping from both sides and the occasional boom from the big guns which fired the "rotten balls."

Gray Bird approached Little Crow, kneeling alongside him.

"I am going to make some fire arrows and see if we can get close enough to hit the top of the wood buildings," he informed Little Crow.

"Do it," Little Crow readily agreed. He was prepared to try anything to break the stalemate in the battle. In his eagerness he quickly went about building a small fire while Gray Bird was busy preparing fire arrows.

The first of the wounded warriors were brought to a relatively safe spot below the brow of the hill. Some of the younger boys, not old enough to be warriors, tended to the wounded. They made the warriors as comfortable as possible and brought water to them.

Gray Bird notched one of the fire arrows and ran in a crouch through the tall grass toward one of the buildings with wood shingles. When he was in range he arched the fire arrow high into the air and watched as it landed on the roof. The tinder-dry shingles burst into flames.

Settling back in the tall grass, he watched the flames slowly spread. Someone barked an order and a ladder was placed against the edge of the roof. Gray Bird watched as someone scampered up the ladder, two rungs at a time, and quickly whacked at the burning shingles with an axe.

Gray Bird was close enough to recognize the man on the roof as Joe Coursolle. At least, it looked like him. Quickly Gray Bird notched a plain arrow and let fly at the man fighting the fire. He could see other arrows whizzing around the fire fighter on the roof. Gray Bird had to admire the courage of Joe up there on the roof, beating at the fire. The flames were finally put out and he saw Joe move quickly to the edge of the roof and roll off onto the top of a dirt wall.

Returning to the fire to light another arrow, Gray Bird's attention was drawn to the many warriors gathered around Little Crow, who was beckoning to Gray Bird to join the circle.

"We are going to make another charge on the fort as soon as more warriors join us," Little Crow said. "I want you to help lead the attack."

Gray Bird settled down on his haunches to wait and scanned the skies not hidden by the trees. The black rain clouds were drawing closer. He could already feel the inevitable drenching chill his skin. The arrival of more warriors captured his attention.

Little Crow decided he had enough warriors to make another

attack, so he signaled the warriors to spread out on the left and on the right. When all were in place, Little Crow let out a battle cry and ran into the tall grass toward the fort. On each side of him warriors were now echoing the war cry as they moved toward the fort.

Bullets were singing a death song around their heads. The whistling noise was drowned out only by the explosions of rotten balls overhead.

Little Crow felt something like a bee sting on his leg. A glance at it revealed he had been hit by a part of the rotten ball. No bones seemed to be broken, but blood was running down his leg. It was not serious enough to worry about.

Other warriors were not so lucky. Two warriors near the center of the blast were killed instantly and another was mangled so badly he would soon die. Less damage was caused by the next shell which exploded overhead.

By now the charge of the warriors was broken and they retreated toward the trees and the rim of the ravine. Another shell exploded behind them, hastening their withdrawal.

Little Crow broke out of the grass and joined the others who were lying in the ravine. One of the young boys ran to Little Crow after seeing his bleeding leg. From the folds of the doe skin wrapped around his waist the boy pulled out a string of rawhide. The miniature medic cut a strip from the doeskin, placed it over the wound and secured it with the rawhide.

By now the dead and wounded had been carried back to where the warriors had regrouped. There was no more cannon fire, but the occasional zing of a rifle bullet.

The faces of the warriors reflected the shame they felt at having been driven back by the cannon fire. That afternoon, two more hopeful charges were turned back by the big gun. In the last attack of the day, more warriors were wounded and one gave his last.

Little Crow vowed to himself that the next day he would gather twice as many warriors and return to attack and destroy the fort.

Heavy rain soaked the despondent warriors on their way back to the agency and kept Fort Ridgely's attackers away the next day. The warriors grumbled at having failed to capture the fort, having so badly outnumbered the defenders.

Most upsetting to the defeated warriors was the "rotten balls" which had struck fear into the hearts of all who had been there. It was warfare of a different kind than the warriors had ever experienced. No one was eager to go back and face more of those assaults.

When the warriors had returned to the agency, the council met while the food was being prepared. They decided to send out riders to the Wahpetons and the Sissetons to see if some of them might join the war party for the next attack.

Gradually the spirits of the warriors lifted, despite the continuing rains, as they prepared for another attack on the fort. Confidence flowed in their veins again as they watched the riders return with many warriors.

As the sun sank away on the day of preparation, Little Crow was jubilant over the number of warriors who had joined the force. He was certain that many of those who had stayed at the agency during the first battle would probably join in the battle now.

The rain had stopped but the skies were still overcast as Little Crow and the other chiefs assembled the warriors the next day.

"There must be about eight hundred warriors who are ready to fight," Mankato said.

"That doubles the number we had for the first attack," Big Eagle added.

Little Crow waited for silence and then addressed all who could hear him.

"I suggest the best plan of attack is to hit the fort hard and try to overwhelm them and not let the battle get drawn out. We all remember the rotten balls and how they affected our first attack," Little Crow announced, letting the memory of the cannonballs resurface in the minds of the warriors.

"We will hit them so hard and so fast they will fall before us," he promised.

Little Crow's exuberance was caught by the others and the excitement of the coming battle had touched everyone. Little Crow mounted his pony, spun it in a tight circle and led the others out of the agency on the road back to the fort.

About halfway to the fort Little Crow stopped the war party to rest the horses. He suggested the warriors fill their headbands with grass and flowers. It would help the warriors to blend into the ground cover around the fort. Soon they were on their way again. They would arrive after the sun had started its descent.

Little Crow led the warriors up a ravine near the fort and dismounted. The war ponies were turned over to the young warriors who were not quite old enough for battle.

The chiefs took the warriors and spread out along the perimeter of the ravine. They had ordered their warriors to hold their fire and try to get as close to the fort as they could before they were discovered. Once fired upon, they would make an all-out attack.

Little Crow gave the signal and the warriors disappeared into the tall grass. A quick glance at the fort before signaling the attack revealed new barricades around the fort. Little Crow could see the soldiers had not been idle since the last battle.

The tension was mounting as the warriors crept ever closer to the fort.

A volley of rifle fire punctured the silence. It came from the barrels of the defenders behind the dirt walls. It was followed by a barrage of fire from the warriors rising up out of the grass and charging forward. War whoops and battle cries sent a chilling message to the fort's soldiers. Surging forward, Little Crow urged the warriors on. Now they must get into hand-to-hand combat if they were going to take the fort.

The charge of the warriors was met with deadly fire, causing the warriors to drop down out of sight. From overhead came the bone-chilling screams of the big guns. The forward motion of the warriors was suddenly stalled and the war cries died out as the exploding shells hit the ground.

Little Crow saw the warriors falling back toward the ravine. He hurried back himself to keep the warriors from leaving the battle. Near the ravine he yelled as loud as he could for the warriors to dig in and fire on the fort. His cry was heard by the others and soon they were laying down their own deadly fire on the soldiers.

The afternoon wore on with sporadic fire coming from both

sides. Cannon fire came at intervals to remind the attackers of its deadly force.

Little Crow could see that the fighting had again reached a stalemate. The warriors would run out of powder and shot if they kept up with this for the rest of the day.

Falling back to the ravine, Little Crow sent a warrior to find Chief Mankato and return with him. It was obvious that the battle plan needed a new course. While he was waiting for Mankato, he thought back to other battles he had fought, searching for ideas that might work here to take the fort. The only idea he could dredge up was to try to hit the fort at a single point and get in close for hand-to-hand fighting. If they could take a building in close, they might have a chance to funnel through that spot and take more buildings.

Little Crow glanced to his left and saw the runner returning with Mankato. Little Crow seated himself and motioned for Mankato to join him. Mankato was respected by all who knew him as a courageous fighter.

"We are at a standstill in our effort to take this fort, Mankato," Little Crow reported. "We must do something different, and do it soon."

Mankato nodded in agreement.

Little Crow described his plan to attack at a single point with a great number of warriors.

"I have been giving that idea some thought myself," Mankato said. "If we can just get a foothold in close we just may take this fort. I would like to lead the attack myself, Little Crow."

"You are a great battle warrior, Mankato. You should lead the attack," Little Crow agreed. "My leg wound prevents me from moving around as I would like, so I will stay here and do what I can."

Mankato returned to his warriors and relayed the plan to attack. The first target would be the south stable. From there, they would pick the next.

Waiting no longer, Mankato let out a blood-chilling battle cry and moved rapidly through the tall grass. Other warriors added their whoops and followed Mankato. Lurching from side to side, Mankato moved forward, not wanting to give any soldier a predictable target for very long. Suddenly the stable was right in front of him. To his right and left others joined him next to the wall as well.

Before Mankato could decide on the building to move to next, his thoughts were shattered by cannon shells bursting nearby. The soldiers laid down a deadly barrage of fire. The stable suddenly erupted in fire as a direct hit shattered the far wall.

The cannon fire and whizzing bullets were causing chaos and confusions among the warriors. Mankato knew that if they stayed there, he would lose many warriors to the deadly cannon fire.

With a waving arm Mankato directed those who could see him to retreat. He moved off at an angle, trying to get to the sutler's house. As they approached it, the house suffered a direct hit and was mostly demolished in front of their eyes.

Turning once more, Mankato started for the ravine. It was plainly the only safe haven at the moment.

Most of the warriors were by now totally disheartened. To add to their misery every cannon seemed to be aimed in their direction. A terrific barrage was pelting down all around them.

Little Crow was loathe to lose any more warriors, so he signaled for everyone to fall back and out of range of the cannons. Runners were sent out to bring back any warriors who had missed the signal to retreat.

Mankato's face mirrored the disgust he felt.

"We have nothing to stop the rotten balls, and they are what keep making us withdraw each time," he said.

Little Crow nodded in agreement and placed his hand on Mankato's shoulder in understanding.

"Let us return to the agency and make plans for tomorrow," Little Crow announced. They gathered the dead and wounded and headed for their horses.

Little Crow's leg injury prevented him from continuing to lead the warfare himself, and he delegated the battlefield leadership to Wabasha. Instead of attacking Fort Ridgely again the next day, Wabasha joined Mankato and Big Eagle in a second attack on New Ulm.

Second Attack on New Ulm

Wabasha willingly took over as leader for the wounded Little Crow. He smiled to himself as he watched from cover on the north bank of the Minnesota River across from the town of New Ulm. The ruse had worked. The smoke from the fires set by some of his warriors caused a lot of excitement in the German village on the opposite bank. It was the village of the Bad Mouthers.

The fires had been set to give the impression that Fort Ridgely had fallen to the Dakota. Wabasha had given orders to add grass to the first to give off great billows of smoke.

The villagers were busy under the morning sun setting up fortifications for the expected second attack from the Dakota. Wabasha could see some of the defenders running here and there in great excitement.

In a short space of time he could see a group of village horsemen gathering, ready to ride out. Wabasha's warriors were behind him in a grove of trees, waiting to charge.

He expected the Bad Mouthers would guess the attack would come from the north side of the river. About seventy some riders proved him right, as they charged down the riverbank toward the bridge.

Wabasha quickly fell back out of sight and ran to join his warriors. Mounting his bay war pony, he led the warriors toward the bridge. They moved slowly, waiting for the loud clatter the defenders' horses would make as they crossed the bridge.

At the instant he could hear the hoof beats muffled in the dirt, Wabasha let out a war cry and charged. He was echoed by his warriors, who sprang their mounts forward to charge and fire at the white riders.

The shock of the quick attack caused momentary confusion among the whites. Cut off from retreating back across the river, the settlers quickly traveled east. Their leader got his men regrouped and they returned fire on the Dakota. The fighting settled down to a somewhat orderly retreat by the defenders as they worked their way east.

Wabasha was careful not to push his warriors too fast. There was no reason to get some of his warriors killed. They had already accomplished what they had set out to do. They had drawn defenders away from the town.

Meanwhile, Mankato and Big Eagle had assembled their warriors just west of town. They were waiting for the firing of guns that would tell them the smoke ruse had worked. Behind them were more than five hundred warriors, not counting those with Chief Mankato.

It was an awesome looking band of warriors, astride their war-painted ponies. This was another chance for the long-oppressed natives to vent their feelings. The arrogance of the greedy whites had been hard to swallow for so long.

Far on the other side of the river, the sudden burst of rifle fire brought a thin smile to the lips of Mankato. Big Eagle met his gaze with a nod of his head and imparted a message. Now it is our turn.

South and west of the town, the land was marked by two graduated terraces that ended in trees clear to the top of the hill. Mankato took the lead and rode toward the upper terrace with the warriors strung out behind him. Big Eagle held back with the warriors under his command until Mankato's had passed. Slowly, the mass of warriors picked their horses up into a trot. Forming into a half circle they fanned out above the town.

Looking over his shoulder, Mankato could not help but admire the colorful string of riders behind him. He remembered years past when their enemy was the tribes to the north. Many of those encounters had been disputes over hunting grounds, not a fight for their very existence.

Sensing that the warriors must by now be all in place, Mankato raised his rifle overhead and charged. His blood-curdling cry was repeated by others as they swooped down toward the town.

On the lower terrace, a number of whites came from the buildings, fired at the oncoming Dakota, then turned tail and ran. As they fled back through the outer line of buildings, the warriors yells grew in a crescendo. The warriors turned their ponies over to the horse holders and charged forward. Immediately, the Dakota occupied the unsecured buildings and fired from the windows at the fleeing settlers.

Mankato rode back along the line of warriors who had settled down to loading and firing at the defenders. Moving ever close to the buildings, they vented their fury on the town.

A careless defender raised himself up, exposing his upper body. He paid for his carelessness as a bullet knocked him over backward. Mankato knew these were not regular soldiers and they would pay for any carelessness.

Moving further along the firing line, Mankato saw some of the warriors pinned down. Scanning the area in front of them, Mankato spied townsmen who were up in a large tower with a big wheel on it that made water as the wheel turned. It was a well-protected place to fire from. He could see it held back the advance on the barricades. To move any closer was to ask for a bullet.

Wabasha had launched an attack from across the river, drawing fire from the barricades on the north side of town. Slowing the warriors was the open ground where buildings had once sat. The townsmen had burned them to prevent the warriors from using the houses as protective covering as they advanced.

Foot by foot, the Dakota completely surrounded the town. Wabasha, with his warriors, held the north side while Mankato and Big Eagle's warriors surrounded the rest.

Mankato rode up to Big Eagle and posed a question.

"Why don't we fire some of the deserted buildings still standing along the river on the west side? We could attack in the smoke that would be carried on the wind through the town," he suggested.

"We have nothing to lose by trying," replied Big Eagle. "I will ride behind the firing line and take every fourth warrior with me for the charge."

Immediately, he chose his first warrior and continued down the line selecting more. By the time he reached the west corner of the town nearest the river he had about sixty warriors. Some had sought their war ponies, preferring to ride in the attack.

Big Eagle shouted and rode toward the town with the others right behind him. The screaming of the warriors became louder and louder as they worked themselves into a frenzy.

A barrage of rifle fire from behind the barricades spun five warriors around in their tracks and knocked them to the ground. Big Eagle could see three were wounded and two looked like their fighting days were over. He urged the rest on, and they slowly moved forward.

The overpowering fire soon bogged the attack down and the Dakota slowly pulled back. It would be sure death to continue further. The defenders had made a gallant stand that Big Eagle had to admire. Retreating, they found whatever shelter they could from the flying bullets.

The fight settled down into sporadic firing from both sides. The sun slowly inched its way down, heralding the end of another day.

A surprise was dealt the warriors when the townsmen jumped over the barricades and charged right into the line of warriors. The screams and yells from both sides filled the air. Some warriors and townsmen grappled in hand-to-hand combat. The knives and tomahawks of the warriors were deadly and the townsmen soon fell back.

Once again the battle became a war of sniping at each other. This continued until nightfall. Some of the warriors fell back out of bullet range to rest and eat some dried meat or whatever was in their war bags.

Enough small fires were built to let the town know they were still out there. Behind the barricades small fires were strategically placed to allow people to move about without being mistaken for the enemy. It was going to be a long night for both sides, especially for the wounded.

Mankato sent a runner around to the north side to bring Wabasha in for a council. Big Eagle sat looking into a small fire, showing no emotion.

It wasn't long before Wabasha joined them. As he seated himself, he pulled out an old pipe. Pulling an ember from the fire, he lit his pipe.

"There are a lot more people in this town than they had four suns ago when the first attack took place," Big Eagle said.

"They had time for more fighters to join them," Wabasha added.

"You both know there are excuses for a poor showing in battle. Our warriors fought bravely enough. With the enemy dug in as they were, they became very hard to hit. When we charge them we are exposed. Because of that, we cannot fault our warriors too much. I think they fought bravely," Mankato said. "In the morning we will try again to see if our medicine is stronger."

Big Eagle and Wabasha left Mankato and returned to their braves. Mankato hunkered down and stared into the burning coals in front of him, wondering what a new day would bring. The grim look on his face suggested he didn't feel tomorrow would be much better.

The night passed without incident. Before dawn, warriors moved up closer to the town, seeking cover from which to fire on the town. The townspeople could be heard moving about. Mankato figured they were reinforcing their position.

It was getting light out when the first shot rang out and there was a cry from behind the barricades. Some Dakota had scored a hit on a careless morning riser.

Firing from both sides split the quiet of the morning. The angry singing of the bullets sounded like disturbed bees on the attack.

It was obvious to Wabasha that nothing had changed overnight. It was a stalemate battle. He knew the might as well leave and go back to the agency. There would still be chances to redeem themselves another day.

Accordingly he sent out runners to have all the warriors withdraw from the field of battle. One of his own clansmen brought his pony, which he mounted and led the way toward the agency. He held his head high. There was still honor in putting up a good fight, even in defeat.

Dakotas and Captives Move North

The failure of Little Crow and his band to seize Fort Ridgely and New Ulm was the beginning of the end. Had he been able to muster at one time all of the hostiles under his command, he most likely would have won both battles. They would have then been able to drive the white settlers east across the Mississippi River. Little Crow also knew that victory would be short-lived. He knew full well the power of the whites. On his trips to Washington City he had learned first-hand their numbers and saw for himself their arsenals for waging war.

After the first murders had been committed at Acton, the Dakota knew they had nothing to lose. Many had their own scores to settle with the whites. They simply left Little Crow's camp and went their own way, raining death and destruction on the whites. The savagery of their attacks attested to the depths of their hatred.

Following the failure to capture Fort Ridgely and New Ulm, the war leaders had decided it was time to move north. They were aware that Sibley and his troops were south of them along the Minnesota River.

Little Crow gave the final order and all the Dakota and their captives moved north. Dakota from the Yellow Medicine Agency who were in Little Crow's camp had been told to move north with them.

After two days of travel, they arrived at the Yellow Medicine Agency, where they found more of the upper band camped. They were ordered to join in on the march, and they did.

The march north was over when they arrived at the Hazelwood

Mission station vacated by Rev. Riggs. The Yellow Medicine Dakota made their camp along the creek west of the mission. The hostiles and their captives made their camp across the creek and a mile west.

Before the afternoon was half over the hostiles returned to the agency and burned any buildings that were still standing. Homes of the mixed breeds living near the agency were burned as well.

Little Paul was a powerful speaker and a Christian Indian. He had been a pupil in Williamson's mission school some twenty-seven summers ago. Little Paul was not big in physical stature, but among his people he was respected as a fearless born leader.

Toward sunset Little Paul and a few of the tribal leaders were gathered together, wondering what would develop next. They did not have to wait long for an answer, as a cloud of dust arose from the direction of the hostile camp.

"It looks like we are about to get some company," Little Paul said in a voice filled with concern as he pointed toward the approaching riders.

Several hundred hostiles on horseback were coming, firing their guns in the air, whooping and yelling. Splashing across the creek, they quickly surrounded the friendly camp. The leader of the intruders, known as Rattling Runner, rode up in front of Little Paul and those gathered about him.

Looking at Little Paul, who was well-known by everyone, he spoke in a loud and demanding voice.

"Little Crow demands that you break up this camp and move across the creek and join his camp. We of the Soldiers' Lodge are here to see that his order is obeyed. If you do not do this we will cut up your lodges and you will be punished severely," he said.

Little Paul, who was by now seething inside, stepped forward toward the hostiles in front of him.

"How dare you, who started the killing and ravaging, ride into our camp and make demands of us! You were not invited up here and you have no right to tell us what to do. Not only will we not join you, but we will take up arms and fight you to the death," he declared. "Return to your camp of insane followers of Little Crow and bother us no more."

For a moment the silence was ominous. The eyes of Rattling Runner, to whom Little Paul had spoken, seemed likely to bulge from his head. Rattling Runner jerked back the head of his horse and spun it around, dancing him almost into the face of Little Paul, who stood his ground. He looked into the face of Little Paul and snarled again.

"Do you not see how badly we have you outnumbered?" he shrieked.

Little Paul's answer to that was to turn his back and walk a few steps to the small circle of his friends, and then turn again to face the outraged Rattling Runner.

By turning his back on the almost-out-of-control warrior, Little Paul indicated the talk was over.

The cool courage of Little Paul raised some doubts in the mind of Rattling Runner as to what to do next. All of his bluster seemed not to have had any effect on Little Paul. Once again, Rattling Runner charged his horse up in front of Little Paul and screamed into his face.

"When the sun rises again, we will come with more warriors and force you to join our camp," he threatened. With that, he whirled his horse and rode back across the creek with the other warriors following.

Little Paul turned and faced his friends, letting some air escape from his lungs. Looking around, he could see that others were as pleased as he was that the ordeal was over for now.

"That was a very brave thing you did, standing up to those killers," said Gabriel Renville, one of the mixed bloods.

The others in the group looked at Little Paul with admiration. He had always been big medicine.

Little Paul motioned for the attention of the group and raised his voice.

"I suggest that we organize and get ready to defend ourselves, for we surely will have company again in the morning," he said.

Other leaders uttered approval of the idea. Little Paul went on to suggest that they send out runners to the several camps, and to farmer Dakotas nearby, calling them to come in and bring whatever weapons they had and prepare for a fight. Renville agreed and riders were immediately sent out.

Little Paul asked the others to get busy and set up a large teepee in the center of the camp and form a Soldiers' Lodge. Those warriors of the Soldiers' Lodge would make the decisions as to what course of action to follow.

The camp was soon a beehive of activity. Cooking fires were lit in preparation for the evening meal. Some of the older girls were looking after the children and keeping them out of the way of the busy mothers and fathers. Those men not busy raising the Soldiers' Lodge were busy cleaning their weapons and preparing ammunition.

Some time had passed when several hundred Dakotas started arriving in camp. Some were half-naked in their breech cloths and all were painted for war. They were armed with bows and arrows, guns, knives and even pitchforks. Little Paul was busy meeting the new arrivals and settling them in the camp.

The blood-red sunset was marking the end of the day as the cooking fires were allowed to burn down. Near the now-completed Soldiers' Lodge a large fire was burning in the center of the council ring. Gathered on one side was Little Paul, the members of the Soldiers' Lodge, and chiefs. The rest of the space around the ring was taken up by those waiting to hear what the leaders would have to say.

Little Paul rose to his feet and extended his arms, asking for silence. The chatter around the council circle quickly died down. All eyes turned in eager anticipation of what they were about to hear.

"Our Father in heaven has smiled down upon us this day and protected us. You know how close we were to a fight earlier this afternoon. Had those across the creek decided to fire upon us, the ground where you are now sitting would be as red as the setting sun," Little Paul said, pausing for the imagery to have its effect.

"At that time, we were badly out-numbered. Now our camp holds many more ready and armed to protect ourselves and fight if necessary. You heard their boasts that they would return and fight in the morning and force us to move to their camp. We will not do that tomorrow or any day!" Little Paul declared.

An outburst of approval roared from the crowd at the sound of his words. When it became quiet again, Little Paul continued.

"Our Soldiers' Lodge is a message to all that we stand together and make our own decisions. We are not about to join a camp of mad killers of women and children. In the morning before the sun appears to warm us, we must be up and make ready. Those who have horses to fight from should have them at hand. We would do well to bring them in close so they will not be stolen in the night," he said.

"Remember, we must not look like we're looking for a fight when they come in the morning, but we must be fully ready to do so if provoked," he added. Paul hesitated a moment and raised his arms to the sky. "May God continue to watch over us in these troubled times, now and forever, Amen."

Little Paul seated himself again by the fire as a swell of chatter arose around the council ring.

"You spoke well, Uncle," said Ecetukiya, Little Paul's nephew. "It is time we let Little Crow know we want no part of his killing and rampaging. When the long knives come they will look at all of us as troublemakers as it is."

Akipa, a head chief, added an observation.

"As most of you have heard, Sibley and his army are not far away. Little Crow's scouts have told him of their location. Little Crow must know that his time is short, so he might consider giving up the captives. He knows he cannot stay ahead of Sibley and his army with so many prisoners."

In the first false light of dawn, the camp stirred slowly to life. Cooking fire embers were coaxed into flame, signaling that preparations for the morning meal were underway. A sense of urgency was in the air, in expectation of what the day would bring.

Looking around from where he lay on the ground next to a tree, Little Paul could see the cooking fires. His sleep had not been very restful. His concern for the women and children in the hostile camp caused him to turn restlessly during the night.

Rising up, he quickly folded his ground sheet and robe and placed them near his other gear. Fully dressed as he had slept, Little

Paul moved down to some brush near the creek and relieved himself. At the creek edge he washed his face and hands. Moving back from the creek bank, he seated himself on the ground.

Raising his head and arms toward the sky, Little Paul gave voice to his morning prayer.

"Heavenly Father, I thank you and praise you that in your great goodness and mercy you have brought us safely this far. Merciful God in heaven, I ask you this day for strength and wisdom in council. Protect the prisoners of the Bad Hearts, especially the women and children. Touch the hearts of those who do these evil deeds, that they might set the captives free. I ask this in the name of our risen Lord, Amen."

Little Paul's habit of morning prayer had started when he was an early convert to Christianity. Prayer was now as natural to him as eating and sleeping.

Little Paul withdrew from the creek bank and set out for the Soldiers' Lodge.

"Little Paul, join us for a bite to eat," Renville called as he sat by a fire. Little Paul smiled and seated himself beside Renville.

"Thank you for the invitation, Gabe," Little Paul replied. "My stomach has been rumbling, pleading for food."

Renville's wife soon handed Little Paul a wooden plate with fried bread and a cup of coffee.

"Real coffee is a special treat in these days, my friend," Little Paul said.

"I can give up a lot of things, but coffee is not one of them," Renville agreed.

As the two ate, they discussed the prospects for the day.

"I admired your courage yesterday, Little Paul, in the way you stood up to those kill-crazy fools across the creek," Renville said. "Be careful not to push them too hard. The situation here is like a keg of powder waiting to blow up."

"I have thought about that in the night, and I have a feeling Little Crow knows his back is to the wall. The last thing he needs is a fight with us," Little Paul noted. "He must know he and his followers are on thin ice. The tribes to the north and west have not been involved in the uprising. He must know he will get no help from them. He can escape to the north, but not with all of the captives. He would have to move too slowly, and the long knives would catch up to him."

"You may be right," Renville said, reaching for the coffee pot on the edge of the coals. He filled Paul's cup again and continued. "With the added warriors and others who came here last night, they will see a larger force if they ride in here this morning."

"They will come, sure enough," said Little Paul. "And if we can avoid a fight they will return to their camp. That is when we should be ready to give them a visit and make known our own demands. There are animals, wagons and other goods they have that do not belong to them. We shall rock them back on their heels by demanding the property."

Leaving the empty cup and plate beside the coffee pot, Little Paul rose to his feet.

"Thank you for the food and coffee," Little Paul said, addressing both Renville and his wife.

"I will come with you to the Soldiers' Lodge," Renville replied as he picked up his gun and followed in Little Paul's footsteps.

The faces of the crowd around the lodge had not changed much from the night before, but there were some new ones. Everyone was armed with some kind of weapon for shooting or hand-to-hand combat. Most of them had their war ponies nearby. Little Paul saw his nephew in the crowd holding two horses. One of them was Paul's horse, saddled and ready to go as Little Paul had requested the night before.

Paul held up his hands to get the attention of those around him.

"We do not know when those across the creek will be back, but while we wait we should sit down so that we do not look like we want a fight. We will let them make all the noise they want when they come. Noise will not hurt us," Little Paul declared. "If they challenge us, we will face them and be ready. We will make them sorry if they fire on us."

Little Paul sat down, as did most of the others of the camp, leaving only the women bustling about with the children. They would keep them some distance from the lodge, away from the possible fight. Many chose to smoke while they waited around the lodge. It would probably serve to settle some frayed nerves. Others talked quietly while they waited for the expected company.

Confrontation

The morning sun was beginning to emerge. The tense quiet in the friendlies' camp was broken by war whoops and yelling of warriors crossing the river from Little Crow's camp. They were returning as promised. Quickly they surrounded the camp, but rather than ride in, they stopped and seemed to be looking at the large Soldiers' Lodge in the center.

Little Paul and the others who had been brought to their feet by the first war whoop stood with their weapons in hand.

"I think our Soldiers' Lodge has caused them to stop and think," Akipa said quietly. "They can also see that we have more people to stand up to them.

"They have about four times as many warriors as we do," observed Sam Brown.

Little Paul, who was about to say something, stopped short. The warriors who surrounded them suddenly broke away from the camp and returned across the river. There were no more war whoops or yelling from them as they disappeared.

Little Paul was the first to speak.

"I think they have decided that they do not want to go to war with us, even if they have us out-numbered. Now is the time to go to their camp and demand the captives and the property they have taken from us," he said.

Loud shouts of approval by those around him rang out. When they had quieted down, they went about painting their faces and bodies and preparing to ride.

Little Paul and the other leaders and chiefs quickly mounted and rode near the edge of the river to wait for the rest to gather behind them. Everyone was armed with some kind of a weapon as they assembled.

When all who were going raised their weapons amid a chorus of shouts and whoops, Little Paul raised his arm and wheeled his pony into the river crossing. He let out one bloodcurdling whoop and kicked his mount into a gallop as he cleared the river bank.

Little Paul turned his head to see Renville pulling up alongside him.

"What do you think we should do when we get there?" asked Renville.

"We should surround the Soldiers' Lodge and confront them like we have them out-numbered," Little Paul shouted back. Renville's face broke into a smile and he shook his head in disbelief of Little Paul's raw courage.

"I'll drop back among some of the chiefs as we ride and tell them what you said, so we are ready when we get there," Renville yelled at Little Paul. Then he pulled up a little on his reins and dropped back among the riders following them.

It wasn't long before Little Crow's camp came into view. Little Paul moved his lips in prayer, asking God to be with them and protect them. The fact that hostile warriors had turned tail left Little Paul with the feeling Little Crow didn't want to fight them. If he was right, now was the time to make demands of Little Crow.

The friendlies fired their guns and yelled, keeping it up until they had surrounded the Soldiers' Lodge. All the riders dismounted and faced the lodge.

Little Paul handed his reins to a rider beside him and walked brazenly up near the Soldiers' Lodge. Spotting a small barrel, Little Paul walked over to it and jumped on top. He waited for the noise to ebb before he spoke.

"Maybe by now those of you who started this war with the white people can see the mistake you made," he said. "Why did you not tell us you wanted to kill the whites? The terrible deeds you committed will be paid for by all of the Dakota nation, young and old alike!" Little Paul paused.

"The Good Book of the preachers says there is to be an end to the world. For the Dakota nation the end of the world is very near. You know that Sibley is marching this way with more soldiers than you can count. Do the right thing and turn over your captives to us," he said, looking down at the leaders in front of him.

"*Hi ya! Hi ya! Hi ya!* No! No! No!" came the loud shouts from the warriors gathered around him.

Strikes the Pawnee took a step toward Little Paul and snarled.

"If we must die, then the captives will die with us!" he declared.

"*Ho! Ho! Ho!* Yes! Yes! Yes!" chorused those gathered about him.

The wrangling back and forth from both sides was carried on until Little Paul sensed it could suddenly turn real ugly. Extending both arms above his head, he waited until he had their attention.

Little Paul decided that getting the prisoners freed on this day was not going to happen. he certainly didn't want to leave the camp empty-handed.

"There is another thing I want to say to you. There is much property in and around this camp that does not belong to you. In your thieving you took things that belong to your red brothers. Some of them are here with me. When we leave we will take these things with us."

Strikes the Pawnee shouted his protest amid the clamor of his followers.

Little Paul quickly noted that his last request was not so loudly protested. It was time to press the point.

"Have you lost all sense of honor during your rampaging and killing? If you have lost your honor and care not for your red brothers, just what do you have left that is sacred?" Little Paul shouted, placing emphasis on each word.

The rebuttal this time was sporadic and less harsh.

"We want to take only what belongs to some of these people and their families," Little Paul said in a voice edged with great dignity.

There was only a slight rumble in answer to his last request. Little Paul looked straight into the eyes of Strikes the Pawnee. This was not the first time he had debated a question. From experience he knew that whichever side spoke next was going to lose. He held the eye of Strikes the Pawnee unblinkingly. The silence around them was deafening.

The long pause was broken by Strikes the Pawnee who broke eye contact with Little Paul.

"Gather up whatever you and your cuthair friends claim as your property and be done with it," he snarled, "but say no more about wanting the captives."

Little Paul stepped down off the barrel, knowing it was time to take the concession won. He also knew his quest for the captives was far from over.

Sam Brown, Gabe and some of the chiefs walked up to Little Paul with looks of admiration on their faces.

"You can almost feel the tension in this camp, so I think we should gather up the property and get out of here," suggested Renville.

"There are a lot of things here that belong to my mother," Sam Brown said.

"We will help you gather them up to take back with us, along with what anyone else claims," Renville assured him.

Spreading out through the camp the mixed bloods and the Sissetons identified property belonging to them and gathered it together. There were cattle, carriages, horses and wagons. Much of it belonged to Sam Brown's mother.

Soon they had most of the stolen goods collected. Sam pointed to a horse tied to a wagon.

"There is my mother's favorite mare tied to that wagon," he exclaimed.

One of the Wahpetons went forward to take the mare. As he took ahold of the halter rope, a Dakota came rushing out of the lodge next to the wagon.

"Don't take that horse! She is mine," the hostile said.

Little Paul rode forward next to the horse in question.

"I have seen this mare at the home of Sam Brown's mother many times, so I know it belongs to her. How dare you defy us! We are warriors and members of the Soldiers' Lodge and we will take the mare with us," he declared.

The anger of the hostile boiled over and he jerked his bow and arrow from his quiver and notched the arrow.

"I will kill the horse before I will let you take it!" he bellowed.

There was a moment of profound silence, and then there was the click clicking of triggers being slipped back to full cock. With many gun barrels lined up on him, the hostile didn't move.

The scene was like a boiling pot about to boil over. Angry feelings by now were running high for everyone. Wasting no more time, the warrior who had held the horse pulled his knife and cut the halter rope near the wheel. Quickly he walked the horse over to Sam and handed the rope to him.

By now horses had been hitched to the wagons and carriages and the livestock had been bunched together.

Little Paul did not want to leave with haste. He walked his horse around the retrieved property and then mounted and rode out of the camp toward the river crossing. None of the hostiles followed them. Little Paul hoped with all his heart he could get everyone safely back. Soon they were splashing through the shallows into camp.

Little Paul rode away from the jubilation and stopped. Raising his eyes and arms to the sky he spoke quietly.

"Father in heaven, thank you for protecting us this day. Your mercy is always abundant."

Sibley's Scout

The arrival of John Otherday and the wagon train in St. Paul on August 22 created a great deal of excitement. Some of the sixty-two people who had been with the train had stopped off at different locations along the way, but a great many stayed with the party all the way to the city.

St. Paul newspapers covered the story of John's heroic leadership, how he spirited the settlers right out from under the noses of the marauding hostiles.

Many white people, hearing of his daring rescue, wondered why an Indian would go against his own race to free whites. It was not highly publicized that John Otherday was a Christian Indian and married to a white woman.

Two days before the wagon train's arrival, now-Governor Alexander Ramsey had appointed Sibley commander of the forces to fight the Dakota.

Hearing about John Otherday's rescue of the whites, Sibley left word that when Otherday reached St. Paul, Sibley wanted him as a scout.

John left his family in St. Paul. John's friend Noah Sinks said he would look after them until John returned. John hated to leave his family, but he knew they would be safe while he was gone.

John had decided to accept Sibley's offer to be one of his scouts. Doing so, he eventually would find out what had happened to his farm. There was not much doubt in his mind as to what to expect. Most likely his home had been burned out.

The next day, John left for St. Peter, where he had been told to meet up with Sibley. On arrival at Sibley's camp, he was taken to Sibley's headquarters tent.

An orderly entered the tent and told Sibley that John Otherday was waiting outside. Sibley excused himself from the two officers who were meeting with him and stepped outside.

Holding his right hand out, Sibley stepped forward to greet John with a warm handshake.

"I'm so glad you got my message, and I hope you are here to join my army as scout," Sibley told him.

"I will scout for you and later I can go see what happened to my farm," John answered.

"John, the brave deed you did in saving the lives of so many white people will be long remembered. I would imagine you and I both know what most likely happened to your farm. Your staying there wouldn't have changed that," Sibley added.

After introducing John to the officers in the tent, John was asked to sit down with them. Once again Sibley addressed John.

"Would you briefly fill us in on the events that happened at the agencies as you know it, John?"

Taking his time, John related what he knew from the time of the first killings at Acton, the attacks at the agencies, and his delivery of the sixty-two whites to safety. From time to time he was asked questions by the officers.

John guessed the interview was about over, and he addressed Sibley and the officers.

"There is a way we could put a quick end to all of this," John offered. "I would scout for a party of about two hundred soldiers on horseback to go by Kandiyohi Lakes and get beyond the Dakota. Soldiers could come from the south and we would have them caught between us. The same number of soldiers could go west and free the hostages from Little Crow's camp."

John was looking at Sibley when he made the last statement, and was surprised to see the color drain form Sibley's face.

"We will need a much bigger army to end this war and bring the renegades to justice," Sibley answered in a flustered voice.

Then Sibley stood up, putting an end to the discussion. He asked one of the officers to take John and outfit him with whatever he needed to serve as scout. John was about to leave with the officer when he paused to look at Sibley. The hesitation did not cause Sibley to look toward John.

Why would Sibley get so visibly upset at John's remark? Following the officer out of the tent, he was left with a strange feeling concerning Sibley.

John was outfitted at the supply wagon with more bullets for his Henry rifle and a ground sheet and blanket to add to his bedroll.

With his supplies packed on his saddle, John mounted and rode back to the area of Sibley's tent. He would be staying close to Sibley from now on.

Tying Red Horse to a wagon near Sibley's tent, John was about to sit down and have a smoke when a rider cantered up. John recognized Jack Frazer, a mixed blood. Frazer's horse looked pretty well used up, so Jack must have had a hard ride from somewhere.

John extended his hand to Jack as he approached.

"You and your horse look like you have been riding hard," John said as a greeting.

"We have, all the way from Fort Ridgely," Jack answered.

The tent flap slapped open beside them and Sibley stepped out.

"I thought I recognized your grizzled old voice, Jack!" Sibley said as he grabbed Frazer in a bear hug. The two had hunted together years ago. Taking a step back, Jack reached in his shirt front and pulled out a buckskin sheaf and handed it to Sibley.

"Lt. Sheehan has an urgent message for you," Frazer reported.

Sibley accepted the sheaf and motioned for both Jack and John to follow him into the tent.

Once all were seated, Sibley opened the packet.

"Pardon me while I read this report," he said. The only other officer in the tent looked questioningly as Sibley studied the report.

John kept his eyes riveted on Sibley as he read the message. Sibley's forehead creased in a deep frown. Again Sibley's face turned ashen as he finished reading. He looked up at Frazer.

"I assume you know what this report tells me. What can you add to it?" Sibley asked.

"I don't know what all is written there, but I can tell you things are very bad west of here. There has been one attack on Fort

Ridgely and most likely another took place today," Frazer said. "I was lucky to get out of there at night, as the fort is surrounded by Little Crow's warriors. If it had not been for the big guns, I think the fort would have fallen."

"The people who escaped to the fort tell of the horrible death and destruction going on all over the countryside," Frazer continued. "On my ride here I passed many people lying dead along the trail. They died horrible deaths. Most of the farm homes were burned and the bodies of the families lay outside."

"Henry," Frazer appealed, leaning closer to his old friend, "the soldiers at the fort and all the settlers out there need help now, or they will all die."

"It is obvious from what you tell us that I don't have enough soldiers to fight so many Dakota. I have requested from command headquarters and the Governor every available fighting unit that can be mustered," Sibley said, leaning back with an air of finality. "We will train what soldiers we have here while we wait for reinforcements. I have also asked for more supplies that we need. You are dismissed to return to your duties."

John had been listening attentively, and wondered to himself why Sibley spoke only of what he needed to proceed. There were no plans for immediate deployment, no advance party of soldiers. Sibley spoke only of his needs, not that of the people facing death at the hands of the renegades.

John remembered Sibley's earlier look of discomfort when John suggested an immediate course of action against Little Crow's warriors. Sibley had failed to make eye contact with anyone in the tent.

Questions concerning Sibley's courage were beginning to seep into John Otherday's mind. Just how big an army would Sibley need before he dared to march to Fort Ridgely? The more soldiers he had the more supplies he would need to feed and equip them. In the meantime the desperate situation of the settlers and the army would only grow worse.

Once outside and away from Sibley's tent, John moved toward the shade of some scrub oak. Frazer followed John and together they seated themselves.

"How many soldiers will Sibley need before he goes to relieve Fort Ridgely?" John asked.

"I can see where he might be a little careful, not knowing what he is getting into," Frazer replied. "You must remember, he is not experienced in warfare."

"I still think he should send some horse soldiers to support those fighting at the fort. When he has enough soldiers to suit him he can follow them," John said.

"You're probably right, John, but only Sibley can make that decision," Frazer said. "He does show reluctance to do anything but ask for more men and supplies."

Four days later, after amassing an army of fourteen hundred men, Sibley left St. Peter and advanced toward Fort Ridgely.

On the trail west many bodies of massacred settler families were found. Burial details kept busy. The grisly task of burying the hacked-up bodies was more than some soldiers could handle. The stench from the bodies that had been lying in the heat for days was overpowering.

On the second day out, they met some refugees. Among them was Rev. Riggs. Sibley prevailed upon him to accompany the troops. His services could be used daily with the burial details.

That same morning Sibley finally ordered Captain Sam McPhail to ride on ahead with two hundred cavalry men to aid in holding Fort Ridgely.

Sibley was shaken by the tales of the refugees they were meeting, but it didn't stop him from commandeering their horses and supplies he thought he needed. He also sent a messenger back to St. Paul, asking for more men and supplies.

Seven long days after receiving his orders to move west, Sibley arrived at Fort Ridgely. His slow progress would subject him to much ridicule in the press and among the people who were waiting for help. The day after he arrived, Sibley set about training his raw recruits.

John Otherday was glad to get back to Fort Ridgely. Soon he would know if there were anything left at his farm. He wasn't holding out much hope for that. He was glad for the company of Jack Frazer, and they talked often.

Four days after his arrival Sibley finally sent out a burial detail of one hundred and seventy men, after scouts said no Dakota were seen.

Battle of Birch Coulee

Though a few leaves on the trees were beginning to lose their color, the warm rays of the sun declared it was still the season of the Hot Moon.

Chief Big Eagle, riding at the head of his band, turned to observe his and the three other bands accompanying them. Returning from their failed attack on Fort Ridgely, the specter of defeat rode with them. There was none of the usual visiting back and forth between riders as they rode toward their villages.

Indian scouts had caught up with them after leaving the battle at the fort and reported to Gray Bird, head of the Soldiers' Lodge and first in command to Little Crow. The scouts said that Sibley was approaching Fort Ridgely with a very large army. The scouts suggested that at the slow pace Sibley was moving, there was little to fear from his army.

Gray Bird received the news stoically. He knew that he would not attack Sibley's army directly. He would attack any soldiers who might be ordered away on a mission.

With the villages just ahead, Gray Bird lifted his horse into an easy lope, leaving the others behind. He wanted to catch up to the scouts he had sent. The defeat suffered at Fort Ridgely laid heavily on his mind. Now, to add to the agony was the report of Sibley and his large army at Fort Ridgely.

His thoughts were interrupted by a cloud of dust billowing up in front of him. The four scouts he had sent out were returning. Gray Bird pulled his horse to a stop as the scouts rode up to him.

"Gray Bird, we reached Little Crow's village and there were

footprints of horses with iron on the feet," reported Hepan, who had led the scouts. "As we were looking around we spotted what looked like a bunch of pony soldiers across the river to the north. They were coming out of the Beaver Creek trees and riding east. They must have been in the village."

Gray Bird felt his spirits quicken.

"The way they are traveling they will probably make camp tonight at Birch Coulee, where they will have water and firewood," he replied, his emotions rising into elation. "When our people get to the villages we will make plans for an attack. You four find their camp and report back to me at Little Crow's village."

In answer, the scouts wheeled their horses and rode east.

Gray Bird arrived at Little Crow's village, but the pony soldiers were nowhere in sight.

"Hepan, when all have arrived, ride to the camps and ask the chiefs to come here to council, Gray Bird instructed him. "We will make plans to attack the pony soldiers. Also, tell them to fill the wagons we brought along with their camp goods."

Hepan nodded in assent and rode away.

Gray Bird dismounted and turned his horse over to the care of one of the scouts. He wanted time to think and plan without interruption, so he walked away some distance and sat down.

In a short time the warriors and the others reached their villages on the bluff overlooking the Minnesota River. Campfires were kindled to prepare the evening meal.

Little Crow was still away in the Big Woods, toward Forest City and Hutchinson, raiding the white settlements. Gray Bird often pondered what would have happened if all the Dakota along the Minnesota River struck the enemy together at one time. He felt sure they could have taken the fort if that would have happened. Unfortunately, every one was free to follow his own course of action. Gray Bird was smart enough to know that whatever they did in the long run would have little effect. In the end the whites would come in numbers that would simply overwhelm the Dakota Nation.

Gray Bird moved back to the council ring where already the chiefs were gathered. He seated himself in the space reserved for him as leader of the Soldiers' Lodge. He looked into the eyes of each of the chiefs as they looked at him, waiting for him to speak.

"You have heard that there is a company of pony soldiers across the river, moving east. I have sent scouts to locate their camp and report back to us. We do not know how many there are of the pony soldiers, but I would guess about seventy five, more or less," Gray Bird reported. "Most likely they will be at Birch Coulee, where they will have water and firewood. I think we could surprise them by circling their camp tonight with our warriors and strike at first light."

Gray Bird noticed that all but one of the faces lit up in anticipation of striking back at the long knives. The exception was Grey Eagle. He was there only because he was the chief of his band and he would lose face if he had not agreed to fight with the others.

"How many warriors do you want to ride with you?" asked Hushasha, also called Red Legs.

"With your warriors, Grey Eagle's and Mankato's, and those I have, we would number about two hundred warriors. The pony soldiers will be unprepared for an attack if we strike at an early hour," Gray Bird suggested. "Soon our scouts should be back to tell us where the camp is located. Until they get back, we will have time to prepare for battle and eat our evening meal before we leave."

Rising to his feet, Gray Bird walked away, signifying that the council was over. The others left to make preparations for the battle.

The ever-lengthening shadows caused by the setting sun marked the ending of another day. The wafts of air carried both the odor of sweaty horses and the smell of food in the cooking pots. Puffs of dust rose here and there from the heels of the children in their pretend warfare.

A larger cloud of dust rose as the scouts rode in from their expedition. After dismounting they turned their horses over to some young, future warriors and sought out Gray Bird.

"We located the camp of the pony soldiers at Birch Coulee, where you expected it to be," said Hepan. "They are not near the water, but up on top in a poor place for them to defend. Any fledgling warrior would know better than that," he added.

"They must not be expecting an attack if they set up camp in that manner," Gray Bird replied. "That means we have a better chance of surprising them in the morning."

Gray Bird announced that after everyone had eaten, those going on the raid would meet down by the river ford. Everyone scurried to their campfires, eager to begin the attack.

Father Sun had dropped off the edge of the earth when all of the raiding party were gathered by the stream. The warriors were dressed in their war regalia with war paint markings on themselves and their horses. The warriors danced the war ponies around and held their guns high. They were ready for a fight.

Gray Bird raised his rifle in the air to get the attention of the war party. When the noise settled down he spoke in a voice that all could hear.

"The success of this attack depends on our ability to move in and surround the camp in the night without them hearing us. I will personally slit the throat of anyone who gives us away," he said, glaring at his listeners.

"When we stop below their camp, I want each chief to come to me for further orders. I will circle around their camp myself before we move in on them. I have spoken," Gray Bird concluded.

With that Gray Bird rode into the river ford and crossed to the other side to follow along the river bank on the north side.

The river would give Gray Bird the best chance of keeping his war party hidden. The column of warriors moved quietly behind, knowing full well Gray Bird would do exactly as he said he would do, should they be discovered. He was not Little Crow's war leader by chance. Where Little Crow had maintained contact with the whites, Gray Bird had always been a warrior at heart.

The shadows were blending into darkness when Hepan, the scout who was riding beside Gray Bird, lifted his arm to stop the war party. Raising his other arm, he pointed up the bank of the river and made a circular motion to indicate the soldiers' camp.

Gray Bird sat on his horse, waiting for the chiefs to come forward. Grey Eagle, Red Legs and Mankato were soon by his side.

Motioning to Hepan to dismount, Gray Bird dropped to the ground himself and turned his war pony over to a rider beside him. Gray Bird waved Hepan ahead and followed in his footsteps. Hepan had circled the camp earlier on his scouting trip and would know where to go.

They moved away from the river and up a small draw that kept them well below any skyline. They both knew they had to keep their eyes peeled for soldier guards. Soon they came to a knoll where Hepan went down on his belly and carefully crawled up behind some rocks. Gray Bird followed and carefully peered around the edge of a rock. He found himself looking down on the camp. It was about two arrow flights away.

There were more soldiers in the camp than Hepan had estimated. How many, it was hard to tell. The wagons were circled up and the troops were moving about inside the circle. Gray Bird could easily see there would be enough soldiers to keep the warriors busy.

From the wagons west the prairie grass was tall — good cover to shoot from at quite close range. Below their vantage point there were rocks and grass for cover. Hepan grabbed Gray Bird's arm to get his attention and motioned for him to look below them and to the left. Sitting on a rock beside some bushes was one of the pickets from the camp. He sat, as relaxed as he might be on his own front porch at home. Gray Bird decided the soldiers stood a good chance of dying young.

Pulling back from the rock, Gray Bird signed to Hepan that they should move on. Hepan again led the way as they continued circling the camp. The rest of the circuit was uneventful.

The soldiers could not have picked a worse place to camp. The outcropping of rocks on the north from where he and Hepan had observed the camp was a perfect location for firing down into the camp. The tall grass to the west made perfect cover, close in, from which to shoot. The eastern, river side had good cover as well. Gray Bird knew that once they surrounded the camp, the soldiers would have no more access to the river.

Once they had retreated below the cover of high ground, Gray Bird and Hepan moved quickly to the waiting warriors. Briefly, Gray Bird spoke to the chiefs, describing the terrain surrounding the soldier camp.

After some talk, the chiefs decided that Red Legs would take his men into the coulee on the east and cover that side. Mankato would go into the coulee on the west and also cover some of the prairie. Grey Eagle and his men would be above Mankato while Gray Bird would take his men to the north side, where it enabled him to see the battle and fire from the high ground. When everyone was in place, they would have the pony soldier camp surrounded.

Silently they slipped away into the darkness that had by now washed over them. Three shots fired in quick succession was the signal to start the attack at first light. Gray Bird and his warriors above the camp would give the signal.

Circling around to the east, Gray Bird led his warriors up the coulee with Red Legs and his band close behind. Gray Bird listened for sounds behind him, hoping to not hear any. All of the warriors had taken seriously his warning about not alerting the camp to their movement. With the exception of noise coming from the soldiers' camp, it was quiet.

Moving quietly, Gray Bird edged past the position that Red Legs would cover. As dark as it was, his eyes could still make out the landmarks around him. He circled around to where he had seen the picket on the scouting trip.

Stopping below the rise, Gray Bird turned to those behind him. He placed his hand on the first warrior to creep up to him and directed him to pass on ahead of him. He kept sending them past him until he figured about half of his band was beyond him. He stopped the flow of warriors, knowing the rest would take up their positions on his left.

Gray Bird knew that his position was the greatest distance from the river, so the rest of the warriors must already be in their appointed places. No alarm had been raised in the camp below. Gray Bird smiled to himself in satisfaction.

Until the first light of dawn, all they could do was try to make themselves comfortable and wait out the night.

While still tuned in to the night sounds, Gray Bird laid back and was soon lost in thought. His happiest thoughts were always of the time when he was much younger, before the hated Wasicuns had come to their land. How nice it would be to relive the times when he had freely roamed the prairies, hunting with his friends. He recalled the thrill of the hunt, the pleasure of stealing horses from their enemies to the north, and the comfort of spending winter nights in the warm lodges, listening to storytellers and bragging with his friends about their horse-stealing adventures.

The presence of whites in the land of the Dakota had changed everything forever. They did not act like guests in someone else's land, but were soon laying claim to land for themselves. That was the beginning of the end for his nation for all times. Gray Bird remembered the first time he had met a white man and saw the menacing look in his eyes. Gray Bird knew instinctively he would hate them forever. At dawn he would vent the full fury of a lifetime of anger on the soldiers trapped below him.

There was nothing left to do but settle down and wait for first light. Some of the warriors would doze lightly while others would lay awake, thinking about the revenge they would exact on the soldiers in the morning.

Gray Bird's last thoughts before catching a little sleep was how many things were in their favor for the coming battle. The warriors could get to water as needed and could fight from cover. Their women left at the camp would move down the river in the morning and set up cooking fires to feed the warriors if the battle lasted long enough.

In the first light of morning a single gunshot echoed off to the right of Gray Bird. Looking in that direction, he saw a soldier running for the wagon circle. More shots followed and the picket slumped to the ground and didn't move.

By now the soldiers in the camp were coming to their feet but not fully awake. Amid the war whoops a barrage of fire from the warriors running toward the camp dropped some of the soldiers where they stood. The horses in the wagon circle were jerking back on their halter ropes and some broke free, adding pandemonium to the scene.

Gray Bird could hear voices shouting orders in the camp below him. His first shot caught a soldier just coming to his feet. The man fell on his back with his arms flung out. Gray Bird shot again and knocked the feet out from under another one. Some of the horses inside the circle were dropping to the ground. The murderous fire was wounding a lot of the horses, which were squealing in pain.

The scene below Gray Bird was changing slowly. Soldiers were taking cover behind the dead horses and others were trying to dig rifle pits to protect themselves. More and more of the horses were killed as they had nothing to shield them. Gray Bird could see that every time a horse dropped to the ground, a soldier would use it for cover.

The warriors who had first charged the camp were now pulling back and were taking cover where they could. Once settled in position, they could fire. Only puffs of powder smoke gave away their locations.

Father Sun had not yet climbed very high when most of the horses were lying dead in the enclosure. Gray Bird thought maybe some of them had been shot by the soldiers needing cover. A clear shot at the soldiers was becoming a rare thing. The soldiers were dug in and exposing little of themselves to fire.

Gray Bird and his warriors had the best field of fire as they lay above the camp on the knoll. The only thing to obscure their view was the haze of powder smoke that blanketed the soldiers.

Chief Mankato was getting restless. The battle had settled down to firing at exposed targets. He could see that there was little protection for the soldiers from an assault on the camp. He wanted to kill all the soldiers before help could arrive.

Crawling to a warrior next to him, he gave an order.

"Circle around and get to Gray Bird. Tell him I think we should charge the camp. Return to me with his answer," Mankato said.

The warrior crawled away on his mission and Mankato settled down to wait for an answer from Gray Bird. Mankato would have charged with his own warriors, but didn't want to usurp the position of Gray Bird, who was head of the Soldiers' Lodge.

Mankato did not have to wait long before his runner returned.

"Gray Bird agrees we should charge the camp, but he wants to wait until the sun is straight up," the runner reported. "He thinks from watching their camp that the soldiers are short of water. He said that you would agree a thirsty soldier doesn't fight well."

Mankato gave his runner a pat on the shoulder, dismissing him to return to his position. It was going to be a very warm day and

Mankato knew the soldiers' camp would be baking in the sun by noon.

Gunfire settled down into sporadic reports. The loud bang of the double barrel shotguns, loaded with the trader's ball, echoed above the other sounds of the battle.

Mankato was drawing a bead on the leg of a soldier behind the low barrier when someone from the camp jumped over the barricade and dashed for the tall grass. He was heading where Big Eagle and his braves lay in concealment. There was one loud boom, followed by another, and the runner was blown backward off his feet — probably dead before he hit the ground. The deserter probably didn't expect to be fired on from the tall grass. Mankato knew from the way the man was dressed he must have been a mixed blood. He was not in a uniform.

Mankato sensed someone coming up behind him, and he turned to find a scout approaching. Dropping beside Mankato, the scout spoke.

"There are many soldiers, maybe two hundred and fifty, coming this way on horses. They are on the other side of the river, but will soon cross over," the scout said.

The report was a blow to the pit of Mankato's stomach. Whatever was to be done would have to be done fast. Releasing the scout to go back, Mankato made his decision.

Mankato worked his way around behind the position of Big Eagle, looking for the hummock where Gray Bird and his warriors were positioned. He spotted Gray Bird and crawled up beside him.

"A scout came in to report many pony soldiers are coming this way," Mankato told him. "They must have heard the gun fire at the fort."

"I was afraid that might happen," Gray Bird scowled.

"I will take some warriors with me and leave the rest to hold our position. We will try to keep the pony soldiers from joining the wagon camp, or at least delay them," Mankato said.

"Good hunting," Gray Bird replied.

Mankato quickly started back to where his warriors were stationed. As he moved among them he randomly picked out his best warriors and motioned for them to follow. When he had about fifty warriors in tow, he moved back away from the line of fire. Mankato gathered his warriors about him and spoke.

"There are many horse soldiers coming from the fort. They have heard the gunfire and are coming to see what has happened. We will go stop them before they get near the camp," he declared. "When we see them coming we will spread out in front of them. You must fire at them, move around and make loud battle cries so that they will think we have many warriors."

His warriors immediately let loose with war whoops and danced around, holding their guns in the air. The idea of stopping the soldiers excited them.

Mankato led the way, turning in the direction that would intercept the enemy. He hoped to stop them from getting near the wagon camp. The grass had grown tall during the season of the hot moon. The stems were heavy with seed. It would provide good cover.

After crossing a small ravine, Mankato brought his warriors up to the crest of the hill. It was then that he saw the pony soldiers coming. He motioned everyone down in the grass, pointing to his left and his right. The warriors moved out to make a firing line. All they had to do now was wait — and that would only be a few, brief moments.

Mankato decided to fire as soon as the troops were in range. Letting them get too close might give away how few warriors he had.

Rising slowly, Mankato peered through the top of the grass and saw the front scouts were only an arrow's flight away. He took aim on the lead scout, waited a few breaths and then fired. The scout was knocked over backward by the trader ball from Mankato's shotgun. In that instant, the other warriors fired and let out blood-curdling battle cries.

The officers and scouts in front of the troops wheeled their horses, rode back a few paces and dismounted. Some of the soldiers took the reins of the horses and ran them to the rear, away from the fighting.

Mankato could hear someone shouting orders, and the soldiers began firing the weapons without even seeing a target. The war whoops of his warriors brought a grin of satisfaction to Mankato's face. They made enough noise to sound like four times the number of warriors he really had.

A big boom snuffed out the sound of the small guns. The cannonball sailed over the warrior's heads. In return, the warriors laid down deadly fire on the troops, then continued to yell and move about.

In between the cannon reports, screams could be heard as the warriors hit their marks. The warriors kept low enough that the troops had little or nothing at which to shoot. The soldier's style of fighting on their feet made them excellent targets.

A new sound arose above the gunfire. Mankato knew the bugle call was giving soldiers new orders.

Much to Mankato's surprise, the troops were falling back and mounting their horses. The cannon fire had stopped. An uneasy feeling crept over Mankato. Were the soldiers going to charge and overrun his warriors? He got his answer when the troops turned and retreated. The encircled, dug-in soldiers shouted and begged for help.

A feeling of elation welled up in Mankato's breast. His small band had put the pony soldiers on the run. He rose to a crouch and ordered his warriors forward. They followed the troops in a running crouch, still shouting out their war cries and firing at the soldiers.

Mankato knew the soldiers were only retreating, and they would set up a position to defend themselves from what they believed to be a mass of Dakota. He could not help but think of the joy he would have later, telling about the time they put the soldiers to flight with so few warriors.

Having ordered his warriors to spread out, they advanced in the direction the soldiers had taken. They moved along at a steady pace and soon saw that the soldiers had set up a defensive position. They were just beyond a low swale on the prairie, leaving perfect fighting cover for the warriors.

Mankato took a position on the edge of a low spot and fired at the troops. To left and right, his warriors resumed their firing. This drew fire from the soldiers and the battle settled down to both sides firing when they thought they saw something move. The pony soldiers seemed only to be returning fire to defend their position.

A new idea occurred to Mankato. Maybe he could leave about thirty warriors to return the soldiers' fire. He would take the rest back and join the battle again at the wagon camp. That would really be counting coup on the horse soldiers.

Mankato crawled first along one side of the firing line, then the other, picking warriors to return with him. His idea of dividing his small band brought a grin to the face of each warrior.

They would really have something to brag about around the winter fires. Two hundred and fifty pony soldiers, dug in with breastworks, being harassed by thirty or so braves.

Mankato led his selected warriors back to the wagon camp battle and spread his warriors out along the firing line. Working his way around behind the warriors, he arrived at Gray Bird's position.

The subtle grin on Mankato's face told Gray Bird that the skirmish was successful.

"The smile on your face belongs only to one who has been victorious," Gray Bird observed.

"You could see from here how the pony soldiers retreated when they thought they were faced with half of the Dakota Nation. What you didn't see was that we finally found them about two miles away, circled up behind what protection they could find," Mankato told him with pride. "We made much noise and moved about, firing our guns at them. We killed some of them."

"Did you hear the soldier in the camp yell and beg for help?" asked Gray Bird.

"We were too busy doing our own yelling and shooting to take much notice of what was going on behind us," replied Mankato.

"I have counted about twenty seven dead soldiers in the circle, and as you can see all of the horses are dead, which number almost a hundred," Gray Bird informed him, not wanting Mankato to think they had been idle while he was gone.

"It is a good day to die," Mankato shouted, filled with the excitement of the battle.

"True, when it is the pony soldiers who are doing the dying," Gray Bird agreed.

Mankato retreated back from Gray Bird's position and returned to where his band of warriors were at work.

Father Sun had reached the point above the battlefield that brought the most heat to the scene below. In between the rifle fire, the trapped soldiers called for water. Many of the soldiers were exposed to the sun, but unable to move without being fired upon.

Mankato's nose detected the smell of burning firewood and knew the women had started cooking fires close to the river. Soon the smell of cooking meat would be intermingled with the smoke. On the return from the fort, four of the settler's cows had been shot and butchered. Today they would all get a chance to fill their bellies.

The afternoon wore away into evening, and the evening into night. There were still a few shots fired back and forth around the wagon camp. The warriors fired as seldom as possible, just to let the soldiers know the warriors were still there. Wasting bullets on nonexistent targets was out of the question.

In the night the cries for water by the wounded were heard by the warriors. The soldiers were paying an awful price for setting up a night camp without secure access to water.

Finally, the men could hear only the coyotes baying at each other and warriors splashing noisily in the river to torment the desperately thirsty soldiers.

During the night a scout had reported to Gray Bird that Sibley had arrived at the pony soldiers' camp to the west. Gray Bird sent the scout on to warn Mankato to pull his warriors from the west back to the main body.

Gray Bird expected that the morning quiet would soon be disrupted by the approach of Sibley and his army. The scouts who had watched his army move west from St. Paul had made fun of how slowly Sibley traveled west to Fort Ridgely. There was no fear of being run down by Wahpetonhouska, as Sibley was sometimes called. Sibley certainly had no concern for the wounded and thirsty troops below Gray Bird's position.

True to expectations, Sibley and his large army started late in the morning to rescue the soldiers. They moved in slowly like a huge, long snake.

Gray Bird moved his warriors away from the battleground, as

did the other chiefs. They met south of the river and moved west to the old villages. Gray Bird mused to himself that they surely had won the battle, but he also knew they would lose the war.

Battle of Lone Tree Lake

Early morning found Little Crow's camp crier issuing a decree to all from the Soldiers' Lodge. Warriors of the Soldiers' Lodge intended to attack Sibley and his army at Lone Tree Lake. Everyone was ordered to go, including those friendly to the whites. Many gifts were promised to those who brought back scalps of Sibley or other officials.

Little Paul and his nephew, Solomon Two Stars, were sitting by a fire, enjoying a cup of coffee. Little Paul watched the crier move on down through the camp.

"Does Little Crow really think we will join him in fighting Sibley's army?" Little Paul asked in disbelief. "He can demand all he wants, but that is all the good it will do him or the Soldiers' Lodge."

"Some of us will have to go with them or we may have more trouble before they ever leave," Two Stars answered.

For a few moments Little Paul seemed lost in thought. Taking another sip of coffee, he spoke up.

"Maybe this attack on Sibley's army will give us the chance we need to get the captives away from his camp. Most likely Little Crow will camp tonight close to Lone Tree Lake where the scouts say the army is located. He will then most likely plan his attack.

"I think you are probably right," Two Stars replied, "but we can never be sure just what that bunch of cutthroats will do."

"Many of us could go along as ordered and then slip away in the dark and return here. It would be easy to take the captives away from the guards and move them to another camp," Little Paul said.

"Those of us who remain here could break camp and set up another of our own. We could get ready to defend the captives when Little Crow returns from the battle."

"I would like to go with Little Crow's bunch and meet in council with the Soldiers' Lodge," Two Stars said. "It is important for us to know their plans."

"That is a good idea," Little Paul said. "I will stay here at our camp and supervise the relocation of the captives when they arrive. I think it is best if we tell our plans only to those in whom we have complete trust. The fewer the better."

"One thing in our favor," Two Stars added, "is that more and more of Little Crow's followers are becoming tired of the fighting. I think many of them will join us once we make the break from Little Crow."

"You could be right, and that will break the strength of Little Crow," Little Paul agreed. "I suggest we move about and make our plans known to those whom we trust."

Mid-morning Little Crow and his warriors rode out of camp heading for a show-down with Sibley and his army. The trip would take the better part of the day. Little Crow wanted to be there to scout the army's position before nightfall.

Two Stars and other like-minded friendlies mixed in with the other warriors, yet maintained a close proximity to each other.

In late afternoon, Little Crow ordered a camp set up on the Chippewa River. From there he moved down within a short distance of the army. Little Crow's scouts revealed that Sibley had placed guards in close to the perimeter of the army camp.

Little Crow, Gray Bird and Cut Nose went out to see for themselves where Sibley had set up camp. From a knoll the three hunkered down to watch.

"The tall grass around most of their camp is in our favor," Gray Bird noted. "Now we can get in real close before we attack."

"The size of the camp tells me that we are badly outnumbered, but if we attack in the night without warning, it will be to our advantage," Little Crow said.

"If we had forced all of those in our camp to join with us

against Sibley, our numbers would be much greater," Cut Nose sneered. Cut Nose often gave voice to the anger inside of himself.

"Let us return to the others and hold a war council and attack tonight," Little Crow ordered as he fell back below the ridge line. Mounting their horses, they returned to their warriors.

The war council quickly became a heated debate. Little Crow's plan to attack in the night was met with scorn.

"For a great chief like you to attack at night is so cowardly it is without honor," Two Stars challenged.

Murmurs of agreement throughout the assembly settled the issue. No warrior wanted to think he was fighting without honor.

Little Crow assigned war leaders to encircle the troops in strictest silence. Once they were discovered, they would lose the element of surprise.

At early dawn the warriors had the soldiers' camp surrounded. The tall grass was good cover for the warriors as they lay close to the army camp, waiting for the signal to attack.

As the army was preparing to break camp, the Indian ambush was broken up. Chief Mankato could hardly believe his eyes when some army wagons rolled out on the prairie, headed straight for him and his warriors. Some hungry soldiers had decided to forage for produce in the gardens of nearby settlers. Their side trip startled the Dakota planning the ambush.

"What are those wagons doing moving out without the rest of the soldiers?" Gray Bird asked a warrior lying beside him. The blank look in the eyes of the warrior was of no help. It didn't really matter, as Gray Bird was thinking aloud and really didn't expect an answer from the warrior.

Nonetheless, the wagons kept coming straight for them. Soon he and his warriors would have to move or be run over by the advancing wagons.

Knowing the ambush was about to fall apart, Mankato sent word along the line to wait until he fired. That would signal those nearby to attack. Mankato crawled a little to his right as the wagon came ever nearer. He wanted to get to the side of the lead wagon so he could fire his first shot from hiding.

To his surprise he saw many soldiers in each wagon. Mankato lined up his sights on the wagon driver and fired. The driver slumped back and the team bolted ahead.

One of the soldiers in the front wagon grabbed the reins of the horses and got them under control. Those soldiers who were still alive abandoned the wagons and returned fire while working their way back to the main body of soldiers.

Big Eagle and his warriors could see soldiers coming to the rescue. The heavy fire they laid down forced Big Eagle and the others to fall back. The surviving stray soldiers beat a hasty retreat under the cover fire of their comrades. Big Eagle admired the courage and determination of the rear soldiers to save their trapped friends.

Mankato led his warriors in an attack from the side, fanning out to broaden the assault. The soldiers were firing the cannons at the warriors, seemingly without pause.

Rising up in anger, Mankato shook his fists in the direction of the soldiers and charged toward them. Those beside him rallied and moved forward.

A warrior beside Mankato heard the whistle of a cannonball and in the same instant saw Mankato fall over backward. The warrior rushed to Mankato's side and his eyes filled with horror as he saw his beloved chief lying dead.

Mankato had been struck by the cannonball and was badly mangled and covered with blood. The warrior let out a wail that did not begin to match his grief. Others who heard the outcry rushed to the spot and were completely shocked by the scene. The warrior on his knees spoke with a fury.

"Let's make those soldiers pay for the loss of our great chief!" he cried. The warrior jumped to his feet, grabbed his gun and charged toward the soldiers. The other warriors screamed a battle cry and followed right behind.

The morning air was filled with angry bullets singing their songs of death. The warriors made slashing attacks on the soldiers, but each attack was repulsed by the superior fire power of the soldiers.

Little Crow was disheartened by their failure to penetrate the defense of Sibley's army. He made many efforts to rally his warriors and charge, but was beaten back each time. Victory was not to be theirs.

It was mid-afternoon when Little Paul, Wabasha, Taopi and others made their first move. They knew Little Crow and his warriors were far enough away that any ruckus they stirred up would not be heard.

Little Paul and the others had met in council while Little Crow and his warriors were fading from sight. They decided that Wabasha would take charge of fortifying their camp, digging holes inside the shelters and rifle pits around the outside. Little Paul would take the captives away from their guards.

With the best-armed men mounted and following him, Little Paul rode out in the direction of Little Crow's camp. Having ridden just a short distance, Little Paul stopped and gathered his men.

"When we get to their camp we will not ask for the captives. We will just move in and take them away. We must not spread out too far as we move through the camp, " Little Paul cautioned. "We will form a protective ring around the captives as we go from one tent to another. Do not argue with any guards or openly challenge them. We will move quickly and get out before they can organize any resistance."

Those around him raised their weapons in agreement. Little Paul wheeled his horse around and broke into a lope toward Little Crow's camp.

Elation swept over Little Paul. His heart had been so heavy, knowing that the captives suffered so much at the hands of the captors. With God's help they would have the captives under their protection by sundown.

The short ride ended as Little Paul pulled his horse to a stop and dismounted in front of a tent. His riders made a loose circle as Little Paul walked up, grabbed the tent flap and threw it open.

A guard was sitting just inside and Little Paul reached down and snatched the rifle from his hands before the guard could react. Some of the captives recognized Little Paul as the warrior who had earlier argued for their release. Little Paul directed the captives to move outside quickly to the safety of the ring of riders.

By the time this was repeated at the next tent, the camp began to stir. Other guards were not quite sure what to do, so they did nothing but mutter and shout threats about what Little Crow would do when he got back.

The number of captives in the circle grew as Little Paul and his men made their way through the camp. Some guards brought out their captives and herded them into the circle. Some, tired of fighting, offered to join Little Paul's group.

When all the captives were gathered, Little Paul led the way out of the camp. He estimated more than two hundred and fifty captives had been rescued. They made an awesome noise as they shouted for joy and yelled their thanks to their deliverers.

Many who had suffered cruel treatment from their captors were emaciated and weak. Those unable to walk the mile or so to the friendlies' camp were placed on the horses for an easier trip to relative safety.

Once they were within the boundaries of the friendlies' camp, many families were reunited with great joy. It was an inexpressible moment when former captives hugged and held tightly to family members they had given up as dead and expected to never see again.

Little Paul, Wabasha, Red Iron, Taopi and Renville quickly met and Little Paul asked their advice on what needed to be done before Little Crow and his warriors returned.

"We can dig more rifle pits and dig holes in the teepees to protect the captives," Taopi suggested.

"We must divide the captives up among those of us who do not have families here and see to their needs," Renville added.

"Let's get busy and do it," Little Paul agreed. "We don't know when we will be getting company."

The meeting broke up and everyone went about their tasks. The village took on the appearance of a busy colony of ants. No one knew what to expect when Little Crow returned to find the captives had been spirited away. Many expected Little Crow to return and destroy the camp of the friendlies.

The badly defeated warriors, led by Little Crow rode in dejected single file, and crested a hill to ride down into their camp. Their sullen mood changed to white-hot anger when they found the captives were missing.

Cut Nose became so angry at losing the captives he ranted and raved at anyone who would listen. He wanted to ride immediately to the friendly camp and kill everyone in it. Little Crow shared his emotion, but thought better of it. Little Crow waited until Cut Nose had lost most of his steam and then addressed the camp.

"We fought well but the soldiers had better guns, and the cannon fire hurt us badly. We lost one of our bravest warriors when Chief Mankato was killed by a cannonball," Little Crow reported. "When the battle started we did not have as many warriors as we had brought with us. Traitors among us left the field of battle."

A heartbroken Little Crow ordered his wives to break camp and told them they would soon leave. He announced that if anyone could find his long-time friend Antoine "Joe" Campbell, Little Crow would like to speak with him. For years Campbell had served as a government interpreter. Joe was of mixed blood, and so was protected by his Dakota relatives, and could move about relatively freely. He had served as a secretary for Little Crow in the chief's correspondence with Sibley since the battles began.

Little Crow's desire to see Joe coincided with Joe's arrival at camp. Joe had been sent by Sibley with a message. As he rode in he saw the surly expressions of the warriors. He wasn't sure he would be able to ride out again later when he saw all the angry warriors staring at him. Little Crow was told he had a visitor.

"I have a message for you," Campbell said to Little Crow, not wanting to divulge it while in the midst of the angry warriors.

Little Crow asked Campbell to follow him and led the way into his tent. Campbell's heart was pounding so hard he thought Little Crow might hear it — especially after Campbell relayed the message from Sibley.

Little Crow asked his friend to be seated and they both sat down on an old buffalo hide. Campbell's downcast eyes told Little Crow the message was not good news.

"I have just returned from Sibley's camp and I carry a message for you," Campbell began. "He wants to put an end to the war and he wants you to surrender unconditionally."

A smile crossed Little Crow's face and he broke into a laugh.

"My old friend, whom I have known for years, would now like to put a rope around my neck. Well, I'm not going to let him do that to me. I and those who want to go with me are leaving here today."

"The soldiers have never hung anyone before," Campbell responded lamely.

Again Little Crow said he would not surrender.

"I will miss you, my friend," Little Crow said to Campbell. "We have known each other for a long time."

The two shook hands solemnly.

"Would you grant me one last request?" Campbell asked gently. "Would you let me have any captive you might have?"

"Your friends were here while we were away and took most of the captives back to their camp. There are some they missed, who were hidden. You can have them."

Rising to his feet, Little Crow led the way outside. He motioned to get the attention of the warriors still gathered around.

"Bring to me now whatever captives you still have," he ordered. His words brought an angry response from the warriors.

"Too many women and children have been killed. We don't need to kill anymore. If you had killed only men, we could make peace now with the soldiers," Little Crow persisted.

Reluctantly, the warriors brought the remaining captives to Little Crow, and he turned them over to Campbell. Once more Campbell shook Little Crow's hand and led the captives out of the camp. At the least he was overjoyed to have delivered the message without losing his life. As a bonus, he was able to free the last of the captives.

The next morning Little Crow rode west out of the river valley. Stopping on top of a hill, he looked back at the land below him.

"We can never return to this land that was ours ... ever again."

Camp Release

High in the sky the sun beat down on Sibley's army as the long procession marched into view. The troops entered the area and set up camp just north of the friendlies' one hundred and fifty lodges.

Sibley had taken two days to care for the wounded and bury the dead. Seven soldiers who had paid the ultimate price as soldiers were buried in temporary graves. Thirty some wounded soldiers were given medical care.

Chiefs Wabasha and Taopi, among others, watched the soldiers set up their camp. The sheer number of soldiers was overwhelming.

"It is easy to see why Little Crow and his renegades returned so soon from the battlefield yesterday," Wabasha said to those around him.

"It is also easy to see why he spent very little time badgering us, with so many soldiers on his tail," Taopi replied. The others murmured their agreement.

Yesterday's confrontation between Little Crow and the friendlies had been anything but pleasant. Little Crow gave orders the night before he left to kill all the captives. Had not large numbers of Little Crow's warriors deserted to the friendlies camp, it could have been bad.

"Sibley will soon come for the captives," Little Paul speculated aloud. "It will be good for the captives to join the soldiers. They will be given more food and good care."

In the army camp, a bugle blared and the foot soldiers hurried to fall into line. Officers shouted orders to the men to fall in. The flag bearers assembled with the drummers right behind them.

Sibley emerged from his tent and marched toward the front of the column. The adjutant shouted for the men to come to attention. With an about-face, he saluted Sibley.

"Have the regiment pass in review and we will then proceed to the camp of the captives. We will place the captives under our protection," Sibley ordered.

"Yes, sir!" the adjutant answered as he saluted and made another about face. "Pass in review!"

With a roll of drumbeats the parade was underway. The troops marched with great pride. As they passed Sibley, the order "eyes right" was given by the officer in charge of each platoon.

It was a parade of soldiers who knew that the war was over. By sheer numbers they had overwhelmed the enemy. Each soldier knew that his chance of seeing tomorrow's sunrise was very good.

When the last of the troops had filed by and the soldiers were all back in position, Sibley gave another order.

"Follow me!"

Sibley led the way to the camp holding the captives.

"Here they come," said Little Paul, watching the soldier marching in step with the cadence of the drum beat. Grouped about him were the chiefs of the friendly camp. The captives had been moved out of the shelters into a circle, waiting for the transfer to Sibley's camp.

Sibley marched with his troops into the camp and called a halt when he was about ten paces from Little Paul and the chiefs. Further orders were given and soon troops were flanked right and left of Sibley.

Stepping forward, Sibley came to a stop in front of Little Paul and the chiefs.

"I am Colonel Sibley and I am here to demand that you turn over the captives you have in your village," he announced.

With his hand extended to shake, Little Paul stepped in front of Sibley.

"I am Mazakutemani, also known as Little Paul. I am not a chief, but I have been asked to speak for my red brothers," he said as he turned sideways, his arm swept toward the chiefs standing behind him.

"Your choice of the word 'demand' in reference to the captives is not well received by myself or anyone standing behind me. These captives were taken away from Little Crow's village at great risk," Little Paul said, allowing his words to sink in.

"When the captives tell what has happened to them you will know many of my red brothers and sisters acted bravely to save many lives," Little Paul continued. "From the beginning I prayed for the safe delivery of the captives and now my prayers have been answered."

"My apologies to you and those with you," Sibley said. "My words were not well-chosen."

Little Paul chose not to formally accept the apology.

"The captives are yours, and we will help in any way we can," he said evenly.

Orders were issued and soon Sibley's soldiers were among the captives. Some needed assistance as they were escorted back to Sibley's camp, which was dubbed Camp Release.

Nearly one hundred whites and about one hundred and fifty mixed bloods were released. Almost all of the whites were women and children.

Arriving at Camp Release, the captives were overwhelmed, knowing they were free of the constant fear of being executed. They had known full well some of Little Crow's warriors had wanted to kill them.

Little Crow had decided after all that there was no point in more bloodshed. Some of them were blood relatives and their deaths would have created more problems and hard feelings among his people.

The Trials

The morning air was crisp. Here and there the trees were beginning to show their fall colors. It was a beautiful time of the year. Soon the land would be covered with a mantle of white.

The hustle and bustle around Camp Release on this morning seemed to be almost frantic as the trials for those accused were about to begin.

The Dakota who had surrendered were tricked into turning in their weapons. Among the four hundred were Dakota who were innocent of any wrongdoing. They were chained up with the others.

"Somehow I think this day is the beginning of a bad time for all of us who carry the blood of the Dakota nation in our veins," Akipa said.

"Seems to me, my brother, we have been having troubles ever since we allowed the white man into our land," Red Iron replied, seated on the ground next to Akipa.

"You are right, but with the trials starting this morning, I think we will see even worse times for our people," Akipa said. "We both know that many of our brothers now in chains had nothing to do with the killing."

"Even though we are village chiefs, there is nothing we can do for our people until the trials are over," Red Iron said, "but we can look after the families of the chained ones and do what we can for them."

The discussion came to a halt as their attention was drawn to some military officers walking toward camp headquarters at a brisk pace. Following behind them were Antoine Freniere and Rev.

Riggs, who were both to serve as interpreters in the trials.

"Rev. Riggs may be serving as interpreter, but his job of sorting out evidence to be used against our people must have made him feel like God," Akipa mused.

"I don't think he likes what he is doing, but someone had to do it," Red Iron answered.

It wasn't long before soldiers were escorting some of the prisoners to a position near the headquarters area. One at a time, the prisoners were escorted inside for their trial.

The first to go in was Joseph Godfrey, a mulatto born of a black mother and a French Canadian father. He was convicted and sentenced to hang, but the sentence was commuted to ten years after he became state's evidence against the other prisoners.

As the trials continued, the length of time for a single prisoner's trial seemed to grow shorter and shorter.

On the afternoon of the second day Akipa and Red Iron were among others watching prisoners go in and out.

"The time it takes for some of these prisoners to go in and come out is faster than the time it would take me to go behind a tree and empty my bladder," Akipa wryly observed.

"What you say is true," Red Iron agreed. "I would think there would be more talking needed before a man could be sentenced to hang. When we were told that we could not be in the judging room and not say anything to defend anyone, our brothers were considered guilty already."

"The Wasicuns have never treated our people fairly, so why would they start to do so now?" Akipa added. "The killing of so many Wasicuns finally made the pot boil over. All of us will suffer in one way or another."

In about six day's time the commission had tried about twenty-eight Dakota. It was becoming painfully clear that even the time taken to convict that many was too long to the whites.

The word on the wind was that Sibley was being pushed by General Pope to get the trials finished. The public was clamoring for swift justice after the death of more than five hundred whites. Some said that all of the Dakota should be done away with.

Sibley knew winter was not far away and he made the decision to move the trials to the Redwood Agency. It was humiliating, to say the least, to be chained two by two for the journey down the valley. There were the innocent — who had yet to be tried — alongside those deemed guilty.

The march in the dry dirt caused a cloud of dust to rise over the moving column which could be seen for miles away. The dust filled the marchers' lungs, causing fits of coughing. Water was dispensed at infrequent intervals along the trail.

To add to the misery the soldiers often poked with their guns the Dakota who were not keeping up to the pace expected of them. Sometimes the marchers were struck by soldiers who were themselves feeling the discomforts of the trip.

The march ended with their arrival at the Redwood Agency. Sibley and his army set up camp near a log house that had escaped burning during the initial attack. The log house would be occupied by the military commission to finish the trials of more than 300 suspects remaining.

The pace of the trials increased, and up to forty cases were heard in a single day. No one was allowed to speak up for the accused, and if the suspect admitted being at a particular battle, he was summarily judged guilty.

November 5 was the final day of the trials. Close to four hundred had been tried by the military commission. More than three hundred were condemned to be hung. Prison terms were meted out to sixteen.

One exception was made among those condemned — the brother of John Otherday. John prevailed upon Sibley to save his brother's life.

Sibley honored his request because of Otherday's heroism in saving the lives of the 62 settlers and serving as a scout. For the record, John Otherday's brother was remitted to imprisonment for lack of conclusive evidence.

Now that the trials were over, the next step was that of carrying out the military commission's orders for execution. Sibley and Pope, who was appointed by the war department to head the campaign against the Dakota, both wanted to carry out the executions immediately, yet both doubted their authority stretched that far.

They sent a telegraph to President Abraham Lincoln that included the names of all the condemned. The president then asked for the complete record of their convictions.

When the papers arrived in Washington City, two men were given the task of sorting those who had participated in battle from those convicted of murder and rape.

That same day, Sibley sent about seventeen hundred of those not condemned, along with their families, to Fort Snelling.

The arduous journey of the friendly Dakota to Fort Snelling was easily traced by the clouds of dust as the families rode in wagons or walked. In charge was Lt. Col. Marshall of the Seventh Regiment, Minnesota Volunteers, with a contingent of three companies of soldiers. Major Joseph Brown was sent along as an interpreter.

There was a growing and almost palpable resentment among the friendlies who were being herded like animals. None of them had participated in the conflict. They were only guilty of being the remnant of a proud and once-free Dakota nation.

The four-mile long train of wagons and walkers moved steadily in the direction of Henderson. The older, more-traveled Dakota knew they were taking the long route. Henderson was northeast of the Redwood Agency.

On the eleventh day the wagon train entered the city of Henderson to find the streets full of very angry people. The men, women and children of the city attacked the refugees, using weapons of every kind. Some of the captive older men and women, even children, were dragged from the wagons by their hair.

Before the detachment of soldiers took action to protect the captives, many of the Dakota were badly beaten.

One enraged woman from the village grabbed a Dakota baby who was feeding at its mother's breast and viciously slammed the infant against the ground. Too late, the soldiers seized the attacker and dragged her away. The crushed and bleeding little body was returned to its mother's arms.

Meanwhile, toward the front of the column a drunken man who brought a gun for vengeance charged the wagon which happened to carry Charles Crawford, Sam Brown's uncle. The intoxicated villager was about to fire when Col. Marshall intervened, charging up on his horse and striking the gun from the man's hand with a sword, risking his own life and saving Crawford from sure death.

As quickly as possible, those dragged from the wagons were recovered and the wagon train moved out of Henderson.

A couple of hours after leaving Henderson the infant victim of the villager's attack died in its mother's arms. The wagon train stopped long enough for the little body to receive a traditional Indian "burial" high in the crotch of a tree. Likely this youngest of Dakotas was the last to be put to rest in the way of its forefathers.

On November 14, the wagon train reached Ft. Snelling, and the Dakota were placed in a camp along the Mississippi River.

During this same span of time Sibley and his soldiers led a contingent made up of three hundred and three condemned Indian men toward Mankato. Accompanying them were Major Brown, superintendent of the prisoners, cooks and laundresses. Akipa, Red Iron and two others were along to assist in the care of the prisoners.

The chained prisoners in the wagons were bounced about and the trip was becoming an ordeal. The worst was yet to come. The journey finally brought the wagon train into New Ulm, right through the center of the city.

On the near edge of the city the first to spot the approaching train of prisoners were those about the business of reburying in proper graves the victims who had died months ago. Leaving their sad task, they quickly picked up shovels, rocks and bricks and followed the train as it moved toward the middle of the community.

Foul epithets spewed from even the most pious of the citizens who in their rage and devastation wanted to wreak revenge on the assumed perpetrators of murder.

Sibley knew there was big trouble ahead and passed the word for soldiers to fix bayonets. Two columns of soldiers flanked the wagons on each side.

As they neared the center of the city the swell of taunts and jeers from the growing mob was now deafening. Finally, the crowd could not be contained any longer. They rushed the wagons, and with whatever they could lay their hands on they smashed and stabbed at the prisoners. Many of the captives were knocked unconscious and fell to the floor of the wagon.

One large woman, shouting in guttural German, broke through the soldiers and hit one of the Dakota on the head. Her victim fell out of the back of the wagon and because his leg was shackled to another prisoner in the wagon, he was dragged a distance on his shoulders and head until two soldiers finally picked him up and put him back in the wagon.

By now the soldiers were constantly jabbing at the mob with their bayonets to keep them away from the wagons. They picked up the pace as much as possible to get the wagons out of town quickly.

Finally, as they left the town proper, the mob slowly fell back, wearied, but still yelling obscenities at the top of their lungs. About three miles from town Sibley ordered a stop. He told Akipa, Red Iron and the others to do what they could for the prisoners.

With rags soaked in water, they attended to the injured as best they could. It had been hard for Akipa to watch the chained prisoners being beaten with no chance for self-defense. He and the others who were not prisoners could only watch from their wagon.

Soon the wagons were rolling again and toward evening they entered Camp Lincoln near Mankato where the prisoners were interned.

Waiting

The morning sun was still just a promise on the horizon. Akipa emerged from where he slept among the soldiers and stretched his muscles. The quiet of the early morning was not yet broken by the awakening of Camp Lincoln.

Akipa's ears picked up the flapping of wings somewhere above him, and he froze. It was a sound not too often heard, but Akipa instantly knew it was Anokasan, the white-headed eagle.

Looking up, he could just barely make out the shadowy outline of the eagle as it now soared, circling over the camp. In awe, he wondered to himself what Anokasan was doing here. Was it some kind of an omen sent from the spirit world? As a Christian convert he wanted to believe that not to be true. But there was just enough of the old teachings still lurking around in his mind to unsettle him.

For as long as he could remember he had heard stories of Anokasan woven throughout the tales of the storytellers. Could the appearance of the eagle somehow be connected to the terrible fate of those condemned to hang? The thought alone caused a slight chill to run down Akipa's spine.

Pulling out his well-worn pipe, Akipa filled it from a small pouch of tobacco. He lowered himself to the ground and leaned against a tree to use for a back rest as he awaited his brother, Red Iron.

They had been allowed to accompany the soldiers and look to the needs of the prisoners.

Red Iron strolled up to where Akipa was sitting as the horn-tooter finished blaring morning orders to the soldiers.

Squatting in front of Akipa, Red Iron growled a morning greeting and motioned toward the camp.

"I will be glad when this is all over and more glad to be away from that piercing horn blowing in my ear," he grumbled.

A hint of a smile played on the corner of Akipa's mouth.

"You must be getting old, brother, if that tooting disturbs you," he teased.

Red Iron addressed a new topic.

"It is said that today there is a new man who has taken the place of Sibley," Red Iron said. "It seems Sibley didn't want to stay around to witness the carrying out of the executions."

"That does not surprise me," Akipa offered. "He has not been called a brave warrior by his own people. It has been said some of his own white brothers call him a coward."

Akipa shuddered at what the days ahead would bring.

"I don't know if I can stand by and watch so many of our people put to death," he said. "Maybe Jesus God will save some of them."

Sibley indeed had asked to be relieved of his assignment. On November 9 Sibley turned over his command to Colonel Stephen A. Miller.

At Camp Lincoln, where the prisoners awaited death, rumors and threats abounded concerning the Dakota. Locals were determined to wipe all Indians from the face of the earth.

Certainly very few of the citizenry had stopped to consider that these Dakota were the very ones who had shared their native land with the newcomers. As guests, the whites had turned on their hosts and claimed the land for their own — a foreign concept to the Dakota who had always understood that the land belonged to all of the people.

President Lincoln in Washington D.C. had received the list of three hundred and three Dakota condemned to die. Sentiments in the East simply would not allow for such mass execution. He gave the list to two very capable men and asked them to single out the rapists and murderers for execution. Warriors who had only fought against the Army would be treated as prisoners of war.

Shortly after the fighting was over, Bishop Whipple had called upon President Lincoln to speak for the Dakota. He told of the many injustices served upon the Dakota prior to the outbreak of hostilities. Whipple's appeal would come to play a large part in the President's decision.

Back in Minnesota, missionaries Riggs and Dr. Williamson tried to appeal for fair trial through unpopular letters to the press. Ramsey and Pope meanwhile were lobbying for immediate execution for all those named on the list.

Stories of atrocities, some true, many exaggerated, incited a call for the extermination of all Indians in Minnesota. Newspapers suggested that they be driven into the wilderness to starve. It was a final insult to the first inhabitants of the region, the Dakota.

Frigid cold weather was visited upon Camp Lincoln on December 4. The tension at the camp was beginning to stretch nerves thin. Citizens from Mankato had been threatening to take rope justice into their own hands.

Miller's first order of the day was to assign extra men to guard duty. a small patrol was sent to watch for any large body of people moving toward Camp Lincoln. He was not about to let a mob take his prisoners.

The early evening activities were suddenly interrupted by shouts that a large mob was moving toward the camp. Miller gave orders for his troops to be assembled. Once the ranks were formed, he marched them just outside the camp. He then had the officers spread them in double ranks in a long front facing the approaching mob. When everyone was in place, Miller gave the next order himself.

"Fix bayonets!" he shouted to all who could hear — including the mob — which was within hearing distance.

"Port arms!" he called, giving the next command, followed by an order for two of his senior officers to "front and center." When that was accomplished he led them about five paces out in front of his troops.

The mob was by now snarling and shouting, demanding the Indian prisoners. At a distance of about twenty paces, Miller shouted an order for them to stop. The mob slowed down, but still edged forward.

He turned to his officers and asked for troops to be at the ready. The order slowed down the movement of the mob to a stand-still.

The self-proclaimed leader of the mob, coil of rope in hand, shouted that they wanted the Indian prisoners.

Miller promptly ordered the mob to fall back.

"If you persist in this mob action, there will be blood spilled on the ground where you stand," he announced. "The condemned will be dealt with by a military command, not an unruly mob."

Once again he ordered the mob to fall back and go home. Quickly, he followed that with an order for his troops to march forward. With their guns trained upon the mob, the troops stepped forward at a slow, measured pace.

The show of guns and bayonets took all the bluster out of the mob. Slowly they began to give ground in front of the troops. A few who tried to hold their ground quickly changed their minds as rifles with the bayonets prodded them.

One of the mob suddenly reached out to grab a rifle from a soldier. With a twist of his wrist the soldier brought his rifle up under the outstretched arm. There was a loud snap and the man pulled a broken arm back to his body. Cursing the soldier, the man melted back into the crowd.

When all of the vigilantes had turned their backs to leave, Miller ordered the troops to halt and stand at ease. The noise of the receding mob was replaced by chatter among the soldiers. Finally, Miller called the soldiers to attention and ordered them back into camp. Double guards were ordered for the night and two squads were placed on standby, all to be relieved at regular intervals. The night passed without incident.

The morning of December 5, Miller set the wheels in motion to move the prisoners into Mankato. He didn't want a repeat of yesterday's events.

A thick-walled log building was secured near Mankato's town square to hold the prisoners. They were loaded into the wagons and escorted into Mankato by Miller and the troops. The mob of yesterday was nowhere to be seen. The bayonet charge against the mob had taken a lot of steam out of them.

The next day, December 6, Abraham Lincoln approved the death sentences of thirty-nine Dakota out of the three hundred and three originally condemned. Most of the Minnesotans reacted with bitter disappointment at the greatly shortened list.

Lincoln wrote the names of those convicted of murder and rape on three sheets of stationery and set the execution date for December 19, 1862. It was postponed a week. The execution of thirty-nine people required time for preparation.

The list of thirty-nine names reached Miller on December 22. He proceeded to have the condemned men separated from the others. For assistance, he called in Major Joseph Brown to look at the list and take responsibility for separating from the others those who would hang.

"I am familiar with most of these," Brown said after a short perusal of the list. An orderly came in with some coffee the Colonel had requested. Brown pulled a chair up to the makeshift desk and sat down. Miller seated himself across the table and filled two cups with the steaming coffee.

"When you are through looking at the list, we will go and separate them out from the others," Miller ordered.

"Some of these names are a lot alike," Brown mused aloud. "It would be easy to make a mistake. I think the settlers around here still would like all of them hung."

Miller looked at Brown and tried to conceal his disdain.

"My orders are to hang those on that list, and I hope you will make every effort to pick out the right ones," Miller said in an icy tone.

Miller's army record was clean, and he did not want any blemishes on his record to surface later. The magnitude of the executions would bear scrutiny for some time to come. As far as he knew, never in the history of the country had there been such a large number condemned to death at the same time. He hoped it would never happen again. Miller took a few more sips of his coffee and stood to his feet.

"We might as well get on with it," he said as he pulled on his greatcoat and hat and walked toward the door. Major Brown followed him out the door. It was a short walk to where the prisoners were held.

Once inside they were met by Rev. Riggs. Changing his mind, Miller asked Rev. Riggs to interpret for him and explained their morning mission. Major Brown would still pick out those named on the list.

Miller ordered the guards to open the door. Stepping inside, he motioned for two guards to follow him, leaving two at the front door. Brown followed.

The low rumble in the room faded away as Miller looked at those seated or standing in small groups. He cleared his voice and spoke.

"Your Great Father in Washington, after carefully reading what the witnesses have testified in your trials, has come to his conclusion. Some of you have been found guilty of wantonly and wickedly murdering his white children, and for this reason he has directed that you be hung by the neck until you are dead on the next Friday, and that order will be carried out on that day at 10 o'clock in the forenoon," Miller announced.

A silent pall hung over the room.

Miller continued, "The following names are those on the list to be hanged: Sun'-ka-Ska, known as White Dog."

Slowly an Indian rose from the floor and walked forward. Miller motioned for one of the guards to escort the prisoner through the door into the next room.

"Wa-kin-yan-na, known as Little Thunder."

Another stirred from the back wall and came forward. His red headband covered some of the frown, but not the hate in his eyes. One after another, the names were called out.

One of the names announced was "Wa-si-cun," the Dakota word for "white person."

A man sitting on the floor nudged the teenage boy beside him.

"Your name is called," he said.

Although dressed as an Indian, the one who stood was a white who had been orphaned as a small child and taken in by the Dakota. His mind was still that of a young child and would have stayed that way throughout his life. He willingly followed the others to the other room, oblivious to his fate.

The identity mix-up effectively freed the intended "Wasicun," a thirty-year-old accused of murdering a pregnant woman.

Some of those whose names were called sat stoically. Brown would then move among them and roust them out.

When the name Chaska, or Cas-ke-da, was called Brown immediately stepped forward and tapped an Indian sitting almost in front of him. Chaska slowly got to his feet and stepped right in front of Brown.

"You know that the name Chaska is the name given to the first born. There are many Chaskas in this room," he said in Dakota. "Why do you pick me? I have not killed anyone! I know it has been said that I took Sara Wakefield for a wife. That is not true. I did put her under my protection, but I never harmed her in any way."

Brown's answer to Chaska's plea was to grab him by the shoulder and push him toward a guard, to be moved with the others.

When the rest of those listed had been separated, Miller, with a detachment of troops, chained the condemned one to another. They were then marched down to a building near the city square. The building was made of stone and was three stories tall. The imposing gray building added no warmth to the chilly day.

The impending mass execution was an event of such magnitude that reporters buzzed around the scene like flies drawn to honey. They were forever under-foot, but the military accepted them as part of the scene.

Absent from their reports were any mention of the situation that led to the Indian revolt. No account was given of how the annuities were painfully late and many Dakota were near starvation. No write-up included the facts of how land was stolen from the Dakota through fraudulent treaties, or how the local traders required the Dakota to repay invented debts before receiving the balance of their rightful annuity payments. No mention was made of the land grabs that brought great profit to Ramsey and Sibley.

Perhaps most sickening of all was how the white man came with the Bible in one hand and a gun in the other. They preached about loving one another while driving the Dakota off their land.

Would there be any Dakota left when this was all over? Would they ever trust "Wasicuns" again?

Cold and crisp would best describe the morning of December 23. Father Ravoux and the missionaries arrived early and moved among the condemned as they had done for weeks. Many Dakota were converted to the Christian faith. Some sat with a stoic look on their face, accepting their fate with resignation.

In the late afternoon the condemned tried to raise their spirits with a traditional Dakota dance. The chanting and dancing made so much noise that the guards became frightened. The soldiers located spikes, drove them into the floor and fastened the chains to them, thus ending the dance.

Even in captivity, the proud Dakota were feared by their enemy.

December twenty-fourth was colder than the day before. Snow crunching underfoot had the high, brittle sound known exceedingly well to winter travelers.

Fr. Ravoux and the missionaries continued to work tirelessly among the condemned. They tried to comfort the Dakota for the ordeal ahead. Most of the captives expressed concern for their families, and worried about what would happen to them.

A few said they wished only for it to be over with so they could "cross over to the other side" to be reunited with relatives and friends who had gone on before.

That evening the prisoners were allowed to have two or three friends visit them from the big log house. Those marked for execution had little or nothing to give their friends, other than locks of hair or maybe pieces of clothing or some keepsake. When they spoke about their families to their friends, the tears would roll down their faces.

Words of parting were choked out as the visitors were about to be taken back to their log house. The knowledge that they were separating forever was overwhelming.

It was Rdainkyanka who recorded for posterity these last thoughts of the condemned as he dictated a letter to his father-in-law, Wabasha. Earlier in the conflict, Rdainkyanka had spoken for continuing the war, but submitted to Wabasha's call for surrender.

"You have deceived me. You told me that if we followed the advice of General Sibley and gave ourselves up to the whites, all would be well and no innocent man would be injured," Rdainkyanka chided Wabasha in the letter. "I have not killed, wounded or injured a white man, or any white person. I have not participated in the plunder of their property. And yet today I am set apart for execution, and must die in a few days, while men who are guilty will remain in prison.

"My wife is your daughter, my children are your grandchildren," Rdainkyanka concluded. "I leave them all in your care and under your protection. Do not let them suffer; and when my children are grown up, let them know their father died because he followed the advice of his chief, and without the blood of the white man to answer for to the Great Spirit.

"My wife and my children are dear to me. Let them not grieve for me. Let them remember that the brave should be prepared to meet death; and I will do as becomes a Dakota."

The following day was the white man's Christmas. Red Iron and Akipa arrived early at the stone prison. They moved about their brothers, asking if there was anything they could do for them and receiving simple requests concerning the welfare of the families left behind.

On this day the number of those to be hung would become one less. The officers and Brown decided that Round Wind, also called Ta-te Hmi-hma, was too old to be involved in any killings. He was removed from among the other thirty-eight.

In the afternoon the prisoners were allowed brief visits from their women relatives. They had been brought to Mankato to cook for them. This visit was different because the condemned didn't want to cry and cause more grief for the women and themselves. The prisoners gave away whatever personal items they had left.

Finally that evening there was only the tireless Fr. Ravoux left among the prisoners. He continued his efforts to comfort those who would die the next morning. It was his final effort to prepare the Dakota to face death as newly converted Christians.

The Hanging of the Thirty-Eight

This last day in the lives of those to be executed was, by the white man's calendar, called December 26. To the Dakota, it was a day in the season of the Hard Moon.

In the early hours of morning a few visitors came to talk with the prisoners. Some were newspaper men who gave some of the Dakota cigars to smoke.

The extreme cold seeped into the gray stone building, stealing any warmth and adding to the misery of all. Akipa and Red Iron left their beds early in the morning, just as it was getting light. They stepped outside.

Wagons were arriving from all directions. From the wagon seats, the drivers called to each other that it was a day for justice, and they would witness it, no matter how harsh the weather. The number of people flowing into the town were more than met the eye. Down inside the wagons families huddled in straw, trying to keep warm with hide blankets pulled over them.

"Look, Akipa," Red Iron said. "Store owners have opened their doors to do trade. They look like they are still celebrating their Christmas. Already the streets are filling up with people."

"Do you think there would be so many spectators if it were whites who were to be hung?" Akipa asked.

"The anger of the white people still burns hot," Red Iron answered. "This is a chance for them to show their rage."

The cold drove Akipa and Red Iron back into the prison. Inside, they moved about, talking in low tones to the prisoners. Here and there they were given messages to pass on to family members.

Down in the town square stood the heavily constructed gallows. It was the centerpiece for the event of the day. The nooses were in place, dangling from the beams. The structure was so constructed that a well-placed chop of an axe would sever a rope, causing the platform to fall. The weight of the person falling would break his neck, causing instant death. That was the way it was supposed to work, but sometimes it failed.

The morning hours were ticking away. Officers and others inside the prison moved about the condemned, shaking hands. To the surprise of most, the Dakota shook hands and bid their last visitors farewell, as if they were going on a journey.

At eight-thirty Miller walked into the prison, followed by Brown, who had an armful of leather thongs. There were also two men to remove the chains from the Dakota.

As each Dakota was unshackled, their hands were tied by Brown and a soldier who assisted. A quietness had fallen over the room.

The silence was broken only by the quiet sobs of "Wasicun." In his simple mind, the young orphaned white boy had suddenly realized he was about to die. He had always been treated well by the Dakota who had taken him in. Why would these people who looked like himself want to harm him? He had not hurt anyone.

By nine o-clock the task of binding the captives was done. Miller motioned for the officers and others to move over by the door.

The quiet was broken when the Dakota named Tazoo started to sing his song of terror. Whites called it the death-song. It was a song sung by the Dakota when they were in great danger. Tazoo was soon joined by most of the other Dakota. No effort was made to stop the singing. Even Fr. Ravoux and the missionaries kept silent. It was one of the few times the Dakota were shown some respect.

Time kept ticking away until Miller held up his arms for all to see. The room fell silent.

Miller turned to Brown, who pulled some wool caps from a burlap sack. Brown stepped up to one of the Dakota and tried to place the cap on his head. The Dakota jerked away, his eyes filling with humiliation as he went to his knees. The cap was placed on his head, and on all the others.

The look of anguish in the eyes of the Dakota spoke volumes. Would there be no end to the miseries afflicting them? The answer to that question was the scaffold awaiting them. When the last cap was in place, Miller spoke.

"It is time to go," he said loud enough for all to hear.

With an about-face Miller left the room, followed by all who were in the room. The Dakota were the last out, and they fell into a line between two rows of soldiers who had been stationed outside.

The entourage rounded the corner of the building and was greeted with shouts announcing their procession.

Some of the officers accompanying the prisoners were stunned to see thousands of people in the frigid cold, waiting to observe the hangings. The onlookers stood in windows, on roof tops and around the village square. The revelry gave the scene a carnival atmosphere.

Soldiers with bayonets affixed to their rifles stood in rows surrounding the gallows. A space of about thirty feet separated the soldiers from the cavalry, astride their mounts in a line behind them. A head count would have revealed about fourteen hundred soldiers on hand.

Behind these lines were wagons filled with people. To one side were some ominously empty wagons. They were to be used to carry away the bodies after the hangings.

The short walk to the scaffold was made seemingly longer by the shouts and catcalls of the people surrounding the square. It was their last chance to taunt the Dakota whom they believed responsible for the deaths of family and friends.

Miller reached the steps leading up to the platform and stopped. Turning to Fr. Ravoux and the missionaries, he pointed to a spot by the side of the steps where they could stand. They were busy intoning prayers for the condemned.

Brown also stepped out of the procession and walked to where the drum waited. From his position, he could see William Duley under the platform in the center near the rope which was to be cut. Meanwhile Miller led the prisoners up the steps. He circled around the platform until all of the Dakota were standing under a noose.

The Dakota once again broke out into their death song. Some clutched for the hands of the one next to them. Officers moved down the rows of the Dakota and pulled down the caps over their faces and adjusted the nooses around their necks. With the job completed, the three men left the scaffold.

Miller descended the steps and walked to a position that allowed him to see Brown and William Duley with axe in hand.

For Duley, it was a holy moment of revenge for the members of his family who had been killed during the conflict.

Seeing everyone was in place, Miller nodded to Brown. With drum sticks in hand, he beat out a short ruffle on the drums, and then a second. Brown gave a meaningful glance, and then dropped his sticks to rap out a third ruffle. On cue, Duley lifted his axe and delivered a blow to the rope. His first swing did not fully sever the rope. He quickly brought the axe over his head and swung again.

A short scraping of boards announced the descent of the platform from underneath the Dakota. The crowd and the soldiers broke into one long, sustained cheer.

Miller was horrified to see that one rope had broken and plunged an Indian to the ground. He quickly ordered a nearby officer to grab a rope and hang the man again. Quickly a rope was thrown over the beam and the other end put around the Indian's neck, and he was pulled back up beside the others. The end of the rope was tied off to a corner post.

Not all of the Dakota had died swiftly, but within a few minutes all were hanging still. It was over.

Red Iron and Akipa had joined the Dakota women who had been accorded a place to attend the executions. As a safeguard soldiers had been ordered to stand close by to protect the women.

The Dakota women had been keening in their misery over their loved ones about to die. When the platform fell from under their men, their voices rose in shrieking squeals.

A respectful time later, Red Iron spoke to Akipa.

"Let's take these women back over to safety near our quarters," he suggested.

"Yes," Akipa answered, "Let's get these people away from here."

Both of the men were too filled with emotion to talk.

Akipa and Red Iron had been told that the bodies would be disposed of by the army. They would not be allowed to take them away for burial in their own manner. Was there no end to the degradation heaped upon the Dakota?

After Red Iron and Akipa placed the Dakota women back in the supervision of the soldiers, they watched from a distance to see where the bodies were taken. They hid in the brush and watched a contingent of soldiers bury their dead brothers in a shallow grave on a sandbar of the Minnesota River. That night, long after the two chiefs had departed, the bodies were dug up and hauled away. The bodies became cadavers for medical training — the final insult for the Dakota.

The morning after the hanging Red Iron and Akipa arose from their beds among the soldiers. They both had made a practice for years of greeting the day out in the open with a pipe full of tobacco.

Pipes filled and lit, the two walked outside. They moved around the corner of the building that overlooked the gallows and city square.

"Look!" Akipa uttered in a voice of awe.

High over the gallows were many eagles soaring high in the sky. They would sweep down over the city and then unlock their wings to climb high again. All of the eagles were following the same pattern of flight.

There was a long pause as the two beheld the sight of their revered eagles circling in the sky. Finally Red Iron spoke in a trembling voice.

"My count of the Anokasan is equal to the number of Dakota who died here one sun ago. I think they are telling us that those who were hung have crossed over and are happy in the spirit world."

"I have never seen so many Anokasan at one time in my life," Akipa said softly in a voice filled with awe.

"Who knows what is in store for us of the Dakota. Maybe the Anokasan knows. It is a good thing that they cannot speak to us in words," Red Iron said.

Akipa gave an involuntary shudder from the cold as he watched the Anokasan soar above. Tears came to his eyes and froze on his eyelids before they could fall to his cheek. Then he addressed Red Iron.

"Little Crow spoke the truth when he said, 'you are fools! You will die like the rabbits when the hungry wolves hunt them in the Hard Moon.'"

Epilogue

The United States government awarded John Otherday twenty-five hundred dollars upon completion of his heroic service. With that money he purchased a farm near Henderson in Minnesota. His attempt at farming fell short and he moved his family to the Sisseton Reservation. There he contracted tuberculosis and died at the Fort Wadsworth military hospital on October 19, 1869.

Little Paul (Mazakutemani), after turning over the captives he had rescued from Little Crow's village, became a scout for Sibley. In 1867 he was awarded five hundred dollars for his service to the captives and the army. His lifetime was devoted to civic and religious affairs. He died at the Sisseton Reservation on January 6, 1885.

After the battle was lost at Lone Tree Lake (now Wood Lake) Little Crow, with a heavy heart, returned to his camp to find his captives gone. With Sibley's large army trailing him, he did not attempt to get his captives back. He left for the Dakota plains, trying to get other Dakota bands to join him to fight in Minnesota. Instead of agreeing to help, they literally chased Little Crow out of their territory.

Little Crow and his rag-tag band of followers tried to get support from the British in Canada, but that failed as well. Leaving his wives and family, he returned to southern Minnesota with his son, Wowinape. While picking some berries, Little Crow was shot and killed near Hutchinson on July 3, 1863. His son escaped and eventually took the name Thomas Wakeman. Wakeman founded the Dakota Indian Young Men's Christian Association, to which he devoted the rest of his life.

The Dakota whose death sentences were commuted by Abraham Lincoln were sent to prison in Davenport, Iowa. Another 1,525 Dakota prisoners were taken to Crow Creek in South Dakota, a barren patch of land. It was impossible to grow anything in that arid soil, so the exiles were totally dependent upon the U.S. government for sustenance.

Three years later the government moved the Dakota to a new reservation in Nebraska. Only a thousand of the Dakota had survived. Starvation and disease had taken its toll.

About the Author

Larry Stillwell was born at Watford City, North Dakota, in 1927. He attended North Dakota public schools there and at Lisbon before graduating from high school at La Moure. He also attended Jamestown (N.D.) College and North Dakota State College of Science, Wahpeton.

Stillwell enlisted in the U.S. Army during the Korean War and served as a instructor in the Sixth Army Food Service School at Fort Lewis, Washington.

Following his discharge he entered a 30-year career in food service management. He was an active member of the National Association of College and University Food Services while managing food service operations at Jamestown College; Dr. Martin Luther College, New Ulm, Minnesota; University of Minnesota - Morris; and NDSCS.

He and his family also owned and operated a hardware store in Ivanhoe, Minnesota.

The Stillwell family spent many years involved in 4-H activities including county and state fair participation, leadership and service activities, and horsemanship training. The family enjoyed countless vacations, summers and weekends year 'round at various Minnesota lake cabins and homes.

Stillwell lives with his wife Donna and their dog Jackie in Moorhead, Minnesota, where they enjoy frequent visits from their children and grandchildren.